P9-DUM-700

THE

RANDOM HOUSE

BOOK OF
POETRY
FOR
CHILDREN

THE

RANDOM HOUSE

BOOK OF

POETRY

FOR

CHILDREN

SELECTED AND INTRODUCED BY

Jack Prelutsky

ILLUSTRATED BY

Arnold Lobel

Opening Poems for Each Section
Especially Written for This Anthology
by Jack Prelutsky

RANDOM HOUSE 🏠 NEW YORK

4

ACKNOWLEDGMENTS

Every effort has been made to trace the ownership of all copyrighted material and to secure the necessary permissions to reprint these selections. In the event of any question arising as to the use of any material, the editor and the publisher, while expressing regret for any inadvertent error, will be happy to make the necessary correction in future printings.

Grateful acknowledgment is made to the following for permission to reprint the copyrighted material listed below:

Abingdon Press for "Thanksgiving" from CHERRY STONES! GARDEN SWINGS! by Ivy O. Eastwick. Copyright © 1962 by Abingdon Press. "Flight Plan" from ALL DAFFODILS ARE DAFFY by Jane Merchant. Copyright © 1966 by Abingdon Press. Reprinted by permission.

Addison-Wesley Publishing Company, Inc., for "The Secret Song" and "Green Stems" from NIBBLE NIBBLE by Margaret Wise Brown. Copyright © 1959 by Margaret Wise Brown. "Oodles of Noodles" and "Tombstone" from OODLES OF NOODLES by Lucia M. and James L. Hymes, Jr. Copyright © 1964 by Lucia M. and James L. Hymes, Jr. A Young Scott Book. "I Am Rose" from THE WORLD IS ROUND by Gertrude Stein. Copyright 1939 by Gertrude Stein, renewed 1967 by Daniel C. Joseph. "Up in the Pine" from BLUEBERRIES LAVENDER by Nancy Dingman Watson. Copyright © 1977 by Nancy Dingman Watson. Reprinted by permission of Addison-Wesley Publishing Company, Inc.

Associated Book Publishers Ltd. for "Sensitive, Seldom and Sad" from RHYMES WITHOUT REASON by Mervyn Peake. Published by Methuen Children's Books. "Green Candles" from THE UNKNOWN GODDESS by Humbert Wolfe. Published by Methuen & Co. Reprinted by permission of Associated Book Publishers Ltd.

Atheneum Publishers, Inc., for "The Mandrill" from CATS AND BATS AND THINGS WITH WINGS by Conrad Aiken. Copyright © 1965 by Conrad Aiken (New York: Atheneum, 1965). "John" from LET'S MARRY SAID THE CHERRY, AND OTHER NONSENSE POEMS by N. M. Bodecker. Copyright © 1974 by N. M. Bodecker. A Margaret K. McElderry Book (New York: Atheneum, 1974). "When All the World Is Full of Snow," "Sing Me a Song of Teapots and Trumpets," and "Good-by My Winter Suit" from HURRY, HURRY, MARY DEAR, AND OTHER NONSENSE POEMS by N. M. Bodecker. Copyright © 1976 by N. M. Bodecker. A Margaret K. McElderry Book (New York: Atheneum, 1976). "A Wolf . . ." from SONGS OF THE DREAM PEOPLE: CHANTS AND IMAGES FROM THE INDIANS AND ESKIMOS OF NORTH AMERICA, James Houston, editor. Copyright © 1972 by James Houston. A Margaret K. McElderry Book (New York: Atheneum, 1972). "Concrete Mixers" from 8 A.M. SHADOWS by Patricia Hubbell. Copyright © 1965 by Patricia Hubbell (New York: Atheneum, 1965). "Message from a Mouse, Ascending in a Rocket" from CATCH ME A WIND by Patricia Hubbell. Copyright © 1968 by Patricia Hubbell (New York: Atheneum, 1968). "Our Washing Machine" from THE APPLE VENDOR'S FAIR by Patricia Hubbell. Copyright © 1963 by Patricia Hubbell (New York: Atheneum, 1963). "History" from THE WAY THINGS ARE AND OTHER POEMS by Myra Cohn Livingston. Copyright © 1974 by Myra Cohn Livingston. A Margaret K. McElderry Book (New York: Atheneum, 1974). "12 October" from THE MALIBU AND OTHER POEMS by Myra Cohn Livingston. Copyright © 1972 by Myra Cohn Livingston. A Margaret K. McElderry Book (New York: Atheneum, 1972). "Martin Luther King" from NO WAY OF KNOWING: DALLAS POEMS by Myra Cohn

Copyright © 1983 by Random House, Inc.

All rights reserved under International and Pan-American Copyright Conventions. Published in the United States by Random House, Inc., New York, and simultaneously in Canada by Random House of Canada Limited, Toronto.

Library of Congress Cataloging in Publication Data
Main entry under title:

The Random House book of poetry for children.

"Opening poems for each section especially written for this anthology by Jack Prelutsky."
Includes indexes.
Summary: More than 550 poems by American, English, and anonymous authors.
1. Children's poetry, American. 2. Children's poetry, English. [1. American poetry—Collections. 2. English poetry—Collections] I. Prelutsky, Jack. II. Lobel, Arnold, ill.
PS586.3.R36   1983   811'.008'09282   83-2990
ISBN 0-394-85010-6
ISBN 0-394-95010-0 (lib. bdg.)

Manufactured in the United States of America   6 7 8 9 0

Livingston. Copyright © 1980 by Myra Cohn Livingston. A Margaret K. McElderry Book (New York: Atheneum, 1980). "Little Bits of Soft-Boiled Egg" from A CHILD'S BOOK OF MANNERS by Fay Maschler. Text copyright © 1978 by Fay Maschler (New York: Atheneum, 1979; London: Jonathan Cape, 1978). "Misnomer" from RAINBOW WRITING by Eve Merriam. Copyright © 1976 by Eve Merriam (New York: Atheneum, 1976). "Two People" from A WORD OR TWO WITH YOU by Eve Merriam. Copyright © 1981 by Eve Merriam (New York: Atheneum, 1982). "Something Is There" from SEE MY LOVELY POISON IVY by Lilian Moore. Copyright © 1975 by Lilian Moore (New York: Atheneum, 1975). "Pigeons" and "Foghorns" from I THOUGHT I HEARD THE CITY by Lilian Moore. Copyright © 1969 by Lilian Moore (New York: Atheneum, 1969). "Ground Hog Day" from THINK OF SHADOWS by Lilian Moore. Copyright © 1975, 1980 by Lilian Moore (New York: Atheneum, 1980). "Waking," "Until I Saw the Sea," and "Hey, Bug!" from I FEEL THE SAME WAY by Lilian Moore. Copyright © 1967 by Lilian Moore (New York: Atheneum, 1967). "The Toad" from CORNUCOPIA by Robert S. Oliver. Copyright © 1978 by Robert S. Oliver (New York: Atheneum, 1978). "Tag Along," "Chocolate Cake," and "Bubble Gum" from ALL THE DAY LONG by Nina Payne. Copyright © 1973 by Nina Payne (New York: Atheneum, 1973). "To Dark Eyes Dreaming" from TODAY IS SATURDAY by Zilpha Keatley Snyder. Copyright © 1969 by Zilpha Keatley Snyder (New York: Atheneum, 1969). "Zebra" and "Lumps" from FLASHLIGHT AND OTHER POEMS by Judith Thurman. Copyright © 1976 by Judith Thurman (New York: Atheneum, 1976). "Some Things Don't Make Any Sense at All," "Mother Doesn't Want a Dog," and "Since Hanna Moved Away" from IF I WERE IN CHARGE OF THE WORLD AND OTHER STORIES by Judith Viorst. Copyright © 1981 by Judith Viorst (New York: Atheneum, 1981). Reprinted by permission of Atheneum Publishers, Inc.

Patricia Ayres for "Sing a Song of Subways" from THE INNER CITY MOTHER GOOSE by Eve Merriam. Text copyright © 1969 by Eve Merriam. "Umbilical" from FINDING A POEM by Eve Merriam. Copyright © 1970 by Eve Merriam. "What in the World?" from THERE IS NO RHYME FOR SILVER by Eve Merriam. Copyright © 1962 by Eve Merriam. Reprinted by permission of the author.

Gene Baro for "The Ferns."

Marjorie Barrows for "The Bug," reprinted from *Child Life Magazine*, Rand McNally & Company.

Kenneth C. Bennett for "Thanksgiving Magic" by Rowena Bastin Bennett. Reprinted by permission of Kenneth C. Bennett, agent for Rowena Bennett.

The Bobbs-Merrill Company, Inc., for "My Brother Bert" from MEET MY FOLKS by Ted Hughes. Copyright © 1961, 1973 by Ted Hughes. Reprinted by permission of the publisher, The Bobbs-Merrill Company, Inc. Canadian rights administered by Faber and Faber Publishers.

Curtis Brown, Ltd., for "Ghosts" from THE GOLDEN HIVE by Harry Behn. Copyright © 1957, 1962, 1966 by Harry Behn. Published by Harcourt Brace Jovanovich. "Jonathan Bing" from JONATHAN BING AND OTHER VERSES by Beatrice Curtis Brown. Copyright 1929 by Beatrice Curtis Brown, renewed 1957. Published by Oxford University Press. "Wrestling," "Follow the Leader," and "Broom Balancing" from STILTS, SOMERSAULTS AND HEADSTANDS by Kathleen Fraser. Copyright © 1968 by Kathleen Fraser. Published by Atheneum. "Girls Can, Too!" from GIRLS CAN, TOO! by Lee Bennett Hopkins. Copyright © 1972 by Lee Bennett Hopkins. Published by Franklin Watts. "Accidentally" from NO ONE WRITES A LETTER TO A SNAIL by Maxine Kumin. Copyright © 1962 by Maxine Kumin. Published by G. P. Putnam's Sons. "J's the Jumping Jay-Walker" from ALL AROUND THE TOWN by Phyllis McGinley. Copyright 1948 by Phyllis McGinley, renewed 1976. Published by J. B. Lippincott. "We're Racing, Racing down the Walk" from SUGAR AND SPICE—THE ABC OF BEING A GIRL by Phyllis McGinley. Copyright © 1959, 1960 by Phyllis McGinley. Published by Franklin Watts. "Homework" from BREAKFAST, BOOKS & DREAMS by Jane Yolen. Copyright © 1981 by Jane Yolen. Published by Frederick Warne. Reprinted by permission of Curtis Brown, Ltd.

Curtis Brown Group Limited for "My Name Is . . ." from SILVER BELLS AND COCKLE SHELLS by Pauline Clarke. Copyright © 1962 by Pauline Clarke. Reprinted by permission of Curtis Brown Group Limited, London.

The Witter Bynner Foundation for Poetry, Inc., for "The Sandpiper" from A CANTICLE OF PAN by Witter Bynner. Copyright 1920 by Alfred A. Knopf, Inc., renewed 1948 by Witter Bynner. Reprinted by permission of The Witter Bynner Foundation for Poetry, Inc.

The Caxton Printers Ltd. for "Beside the Line of Elephants" from PICK POCKET SONGS by Edna Becker (Caldwell, Idaho: The Caxton Printers Ltd.). Reprinted by permission.

Miriam Chaikin for "I Hate Harry." Reprinted by permission of the author. "Ms. Whatchamacallit Thingamajig," reprinted from *Woman's Day*. Copyright © 1980 by Miriam Chaikin. Reprinted by permission of the author.

Chatto and Windus Ltd. for "Lone Dog" from SONGS TO SAVE A SOUL by Irene Rutherford McLeod. Reprinted by permission of the Author's Literary Estate and Chatto and Windus Ltd.

Clarion Books for "Night Comes" from A BUNCH OF POEMS AND VERSES by Beatrice Schenk de Regniers. Copyright © 1976 by Beatrice Schenk de Regniers. Published by Clarion Books, Ticknor & Fields: A Houghton Mifflin Company.

Elizabeth Coatsworth for "Country Barnyard" from NIGHT AND THE CAT.

Joanna Cole for "Driving to the Beach." Copyright © 1973 by Joanna Cole.

William Cole for "Sneaky Bill," "Banananananananana," and "Did You?" by William Cole. Copyright © 1977 by William Cole. "Valentine" by Shel Silverstein. Copyright © 1961 by Shel Silverstein.

Commonweal Publishing Co., Inc., for "Godmother" by Phyllis B. Morden.

Hilda Conkling for "Dandelion." Reprinted by permission of the author.

Mary Elizabeth Counselman for "Gift with the Wrappings Off."

The Lois Lenski Covey Foundation, Inc., for "Sing a Song of People" from THE LIFE I LIVE by Lois Lenski. Copyright © 1965 by The Lois Lenski Covey Foundation, Inc. Reprinted by permission of The Lois Lenski Covey Foundation, Inc.

Delacorte Press for "Lion" from LAUGHING TIME by William Jay Smith. Copyright © 1953, 1955, 1956, 1957, 1959, 1968, 1974, 1977, 1980 by William Jay Smith. Reprinted by permission of Delacorte Press/Seymour Lawrence. "Unicorn," "The Toaster," "Seal," "Love," and "Jittery Jim" from LAUGHING TIME by William Jay Smith. Copyright © 1953, 1955, 1956, 1957, 1959, 1968, 1974, 1977, 1980 by William Jay Smith. Reprinted by permission of Delacorte Press/Seymour Lawrence. A Merloyd Lawrence Book.

Dewes & Son for "Who's In" by Elizabeth Fleming. Reprinted by permission of Alison Fleming.

The Dial Press for "Lil' Bro'" and "Basketball Star" from MY DADDY IS A COOL DUDE AND OTHER POEMS by Karama Fufuka. Copyright © 1975 by Karama Fufuka. Reprinted by permission of The Dial Press.

Dennis Dobson Publishers for "On the Ning Nang Nong," "A Thousand Hairy Savages," and "You Must Never Bath in an Irish Stew" from SILLY VERSE FOR KIDS by Spike Milligan.

Candida Donadio & Associates, Inc., for "Number Nine, Penwiper Mews" and "Lord Cray" from AMPHIGOREY by Edward Gorey. Copyright © 1972 by Edward Gorey. Reprinted by permission of Candida Donadio & Associates, Inc. Canadian rights administered by Deborah Rogers Ltd.

Doubleday & Company, Inc., for "If Once You Have Slept on an Island" from TAXIS AND TOADSTOOLS by Rachel Field. Copyright 1926 by The Century Company. "Mice" from FIFTY ONE NEW NURSERY RHYMES by Rose Fyleman. Copyright 1932 by Doubleday & Company, Inc. Canadian rights administered by The Society of Authors. "Easter" from POEMS, ESSAYS AND LETTERS by Joyce Kilmer. Copyright 1914 by Harriet Monroe. "Feelings About Words" from WORDS, WORDS, WORDS by Mary O'Neill. Copyright © 1966 by Mary O'Neill. "What Is Red?" and "What Is Orange?" from HAILSTONES AND HALIBUT BONES by Mary O'Neill. Copyright © 1961 by Mary Le Duc O'Neill. "Miss Norma Jean Pugh" from PEOPLE I'D LIKE TO KEEP by Mary O'Neill. Copyright © 1964 by Mary O'Neill. "The Serpent" and "The Sloth" from THE COLLECTED POEMS OF THEODORE ROETHKE. Copyright 1950 by Theodore Roethke. "The Lizard" from THE COLLECTED POEMS OF THEODORE ROETHKE. Copyright © 1961 by Theodore Roethke. "Dinky" from THE COLLECTED POEMS OF THEODORE ROETHKE. Copyright 1953 by Theodore Roethke. "The Bat" from THE COLLECTED POEMS OF THEODORE ROETHKE. Copyright 1938 by Theodore Roethke. "I Am Cherry Alive" from SUMMER KNOWLEDGE, NEW AND SELECTED POEMS by Delmore Schwartz. "Could It Have Been a Shadow?" from GOOSE GRASS RHYMES by Monica Shannon. Copyright 1930 by Doubleday & Company, Inc. "How to Tell Goblins from Elves" from GOOSE GRASS RHYMES by Monica Shannon. Copyright 1930 by Monica Shannon Wing. "The Blackbird" from KENSINGTON GARDENS by Humbert Wolfe. Canadian rights administered by Ann Wolfe. "The Pig" and "The Flea" from NOT FOR CHILDREN by Roland Young. Reprinted by permission of Doubleday & Company, Inc.

E. P. Dutton & Co., Inc., for "The Wrong Start" from RHYMES ABOUT US by Marchette Chute. Copyright © 1974 by Marchette Chute. "Wiggly Giggles" from ME IS HOW I FEEL: POEMS by Stacy Jo Crossen and Natalie Anne Covell. Copyright © 1970 by A. Harris Stone, Stacy Crossen, Natalie Covell, and Victoria deLarrea. "How Strange It Is" from POEMS OF EARTH AND SPACE by Claudia Lewis. Copyright © 1967 by Claudia Lewis. "The More It Snows" from THE HOUSE AT POOH CORNER by A. A. Milne. Copyright 1928 by E. P. Dutton & Co., Inc., renewed 1956 by A. A. Milne. Canadian rights administered by McClelland and Stewart Ltd. Reprinted by permission of the publisher, E. P. Dutton & Co., Inc.

E. C. Publications, Inc., for "The Bat" from MAD FOR BETTER OR VERSE. Copyright © 1968, 1975 by Frank Jacobs and E. C. Publications, Inc.

Norma Millay Ellis, Literary Executor, for "Travel" from COLLECTED POEMS by Edna St. Vincent Millay. Copyright 1921, 1948 by Edna St. Vincent Millay. Published by Harper & Row.

Evans Brothers Limited for "Rainy Nights" from COME FOLLOW ME by Irene Thompson.

Farrar, Straus & Giroux, Inc., for "basketball" from SPIN A SOFT BLACK SONG by Nikki Giovanni. Copyright © 1971 by Nikki Giovanni. Reprinted by permission of Hill and Wang, a Division of Farrar, Straus & Giroux, Inc. "Crickets" from SMALL POEMS by Valerie Worth. Copyright © 1972 by Valerie Worth. Reprinted by permission of Farrar, Straus & Giroux, Inc.

Four Winds Press for "Wendy in Winter" from THE COVERED BRIDGE HOUSE AND OTHER POEMS by Kaye Starbird Jennison. Copyright © 1979 by Kaye Starbird Jennison. Reprinted by permission of Four Winds Press, a Division of Scholastic Inc.

Martin Gardner for "Soap" and "Barbershop."

Grosset & Dunlap, Inc., for "Rhyme" from THE SPARROW BUSH by Elizabeth Coatsworth. Copyright © 1966 by Grosset & Dunlap, Inc. "The Sparrow Hawk" and "The Tin Frog" from THE PEDALING MAN by Russell Hoban. Copyright © 1968 by Russell Hoban. Reprinted by permission of Grosset & Dunlap, Inc.

Harcourt Brace Jovanovich, Inc., for "Ladybug" from MORNING IS A LITTLE CHILD by Joan Walsh Anglund. Copyright © 1969 by Joan Walsh Anglund. "Growing Up" and "Trees" from THE LITTLE HILL by Harry Behn. Copyright 1949 by Harry Behn, renewed 1977 by Alice L. Behn. "maggie and milly and molly and may" from COMPLETE POEMS 1913–1962 by e. e. cummings. Copyright © 1956 by e. e. cummings. "Keep a Poem in Your Pocket" from SOMETHING SPECIAL by Beatrice Schenk de Regniers. Copyright © 1958 by Beatrice Schenk de Regniers. "Arithmetic" from THE COMPLETE POEMS OF CARL SANDBURG. Copyright 1950 by Carl Sandburg, renewed 1978 by Margaret Sandburg, Helga Sandburg Crile, and Janet Sandburg. "Buffalo Dusk" from SMOKE AND STEEL by Carl Sandburg. Copyright 1920 by Harcourt Brace Jovanovich, Inc., renewed 1948 by Carl Sandburg. "Fog" from CHICAGO POEMS by Carl Sandburg. Copyright 1916 by Holt, Rinehart and Winston, Inc., renewed 1944 by Carl Sandburg. "The Opposite of Two" from OPPOSITES by Richard Wilbur. Copyright © 1973 by Richard Wilbur. Reprinted by permission of Harcourt Brace Jovanovich, Inc.

Harper & Row, Publishers, Inc., for "First Snow" from A POCKETFUL OF POEMS by Marie Louise Allen. Copyright © 1957 by Marie Allen Howarth. "Keziah" and "Rudolph Is Tired of the City" from BRONZEVILLE BOYS AND GIRLS by Gwendolyn Brooks. Copyright © 1956 by Gwendolyn Brooks Blakely. "The Spangled Pandemonium" from BEYOND THE PAWPAW TREES by Palmer Brown. Copyright 1954 by Palmer Brown. "The Myra Song" from THE MONSTER DEN by John Ciardi. Copyright © 1963, 1964, 1966 by John Ciardi. "What Someone Said When He Was Spanked on the Day Before His Birthday" from YOU KNOW WHO by John Ciardi. Copyright © 1964 by John Ciardi. "Mummy Slept Late and Daddy Fixed Breakfast" from YOU READ TO ME, I'LL READ TO YOU by John Ciardi. Copyright © 1962 by John Ciardi. "A Dragonfly" from ELEANOR FARJEON'S POEMS FOR CHILDREN. Copyright 1933, 1961 by Eleanor Farjeon. "The Children's Carol" from ELEANOR FARJEON'S POEMS FOR CHILDREN. Copyright 1927, 1951 by Eleanor Farjeon. "The Witch! The Witch!" from ELEANOR FARJEON'S POEMS FOR CHILDREN. Copyright 1926, 1951 by Eleanor Farjeon. "Bliss," "Poetry," and "Yawning" from ELEANOR FARJEON'S POEMS FOR CHILDREN. Copyright 1938, 1951 by Eleanor Farjeon. "Merry Christmas" from FEATHERED ONES AND FURRY by Aileen Fisher. Copyright © 1971 by Aileen Fisher. "Light the Festive Candles" and "On Mother's Day" from SKIP AROUND THE YEAR by Aileen Fisher. Copyright © 1967 by Aileen Fisher. "Egg Thoughts," "Homework," and "Stupid Old Myself" from EGG THOUGHTS by Russell Hoban. Copyright © 1964, 1972 by Russell Hoban. "Spring" and "The Middle of the Night" from DOGS AND DRAGONS, TREES AND DREAMS by Karla Kuskin. Copyright © 1958 by Karla Kuskin. "A Bug Sat in a Silver Flower" from DOGS AND DRAGONS, TREES AND DREAMS by Karla Kuskin. Copyright © 1975 by Karla Kuskin. "Me" and "Rules" from DOGS AND DRAGONS, TREES AND DREAMS by Karla Kuskin. Copyright © 1962 by Karla Kuskin. "Winter Clothes" from THE ROSE ON MY CAKE by Karla Kuskin. Copyright © 1964 by Karla Kuskin. "Frightening" from UP AND DOWN THE RIVER by Claudia Lewis. Copyright © 1979 by Claudia Lewis. "Daylight Saving Time" from WONDERFUL TIME by Phyllis McGinley. Copyright © 1965, 1966 by Phyllis McGinley. "When Mosquitoes Make a Meal" from THE WINDS THAT COME FROM FAR AWAY by Else Holmelund Minarik. Copyright © 1964 by Else Holmelund Minarik. "Six Weeks Old" from CHIMNEY SMOKE by Christopher Morley. Copyright 1921, 1949 by Christopher Morley. "The Plumpuppets" from THE ROCKING HORSE by Christopher Morley. Copyright 1919 by Harper & Row, Publishers, Inc., renewed 1947 by Christopher Morley. "These Are the Beds . . ." from THE BED BOOK by Sylvia Plath. Copyright © 1976 by Ted Hughes. Canadian rights administered by Olwyn Hughes.

"October" from CHICKEN SOUP WITH RICE by Maurice Sendak. Copyright © 1962 by Maurice Sendak. "Hug O' War," "Jimmy Jet and His TV Set," and "Smart" from WHERE THE SIDEWALK ENDS by Shel Silverstein. Copyright © 1974 by Shel Silverstein. "Pie Problem" and "The Little Boy and the Old Man" from A LIGHT IN THE ATTIC by Shel Silverstein. Copyright © 1981 by Shel Silverstein. "Sunning" from CRICKETY CRICKET! THE BEST LOVED POEMS OF JAMES S. TIPPETT. Copyright 1933 by Harper & Row, Publishers, Inc., renewed © 1961 by Martha K. Tippett. "Huckleberry, Gooseberry, Raspberry" from FATHER FOX'S PENNYRHYMES by Clyde Watson. Copyright © 1971 by Clyde Watson. "Yip-yap Rattletrap" from QUIPS & QUIRKS by Clyde Watson. Copyright © 1975 by Clyde Watson. "People" from ALL THAT SUNLIGHT by Charlotte Zolotow. Copyright © 1967 by Charlotte Zolotow. "River Winding" and "A Moment in Summer" from RIVER WINDING by Charlotte Zolotow. Copyright © 1970 by Charlotte Zolotow.

William Heinemann Ltd. for "The Hairy Dog" from PILLICOCK HILL by Herbert Asquith. "The Wind," "Mr. Kartoffel," and "Doctor Emmanuel" by James Reeves. "The Bogus-Boo" from MORE PREFABULOUS ANIMALES by James Reeves.

Margaret Hillert for "About Feet" and "Just Me."

Mary Ann Hoberman for "Night" from HELLO AND GOOD-BY.

Hodder & Stoughton Limited for "House. For Sale" from THE SINGING TIME by Leonard Clark.

Holiday House, Inc., for "What's That?" by Florence Parry Heide from MONSTER POEMS, Daisy Wallace, editor. Copyright © 1976 by Florence Parry Heide. "Witches' Menu" by Sonja Nikolay from WITCH POEMS, Daisy Wallace, editor. Copyright © 1976 by Holiday House, Inc. Reprinted by permission of Holiday House, Inc.

Felice Holman for "Sulk" from I HEAR YOU SMILING AND OTHER POEMS by Felice Holman. Copyright © 1973 by Felice Holman (New York: Charles Scribner's Sons, 1973).

Holt, Rinehart and Winston, Publishers, for "The Walrus" and "The Hummingbird" from CREATURES GREAT AND SMALL by Michael Flanders. Copyright © 1964 by Michael Flanders. "Dust of Snow," "Stopping by Woods on a Snowy Evening," and "Fireflies in the Garden" from THE POETRY OF ROBERT FROST, Edward Connery Lathem, editor. Copyright 1923, 1928, © 1969 by Holt, Rinehart and Winston. Copyright 1951, © 1956 by Robert Frost. "To an Aviator" from BRIGHT HARBOR by Daniel Whitehead Hicky. Copyright 1932, © 1960 by Daniel Whitehead Hicky. "Queenie" from ALPHABET OF GIRLS by Leland B. Jacobs. Copyright © 1969 by Leland B. Jacobs. "That May Morning" and "Taste of Purple" from IS SOMEWHERE ALWAYS FAR AWAY? by Leland B. Jacobs. Copyright © 1967 by Leland B. Jacobs. "Steam Shovel" from UPPER PASTURE by Charles Malam. Copyright 1930, © 1958 by Charles Malam. Reprinted by permission of Holt, Rinehart and Winston, Publishers.

The Horn Book, Inc., for "One Day When We Went Walking" by Valine Hobbs, reprinted from *The Horn Book Magazine*, January 1947. Copyright © 1947 by The Horn Book, Inc.

Houghton Mifflin Company for "Read This with Gestures" from FAST AND SLOW by John Ciardi. Copyright © 1975 by John Ciardi. "I Wish I Could Meet the Man That Knows" from I MET A MAN by John Ciardi. Copyright © 1961 by John Ciardi. "Tony Baloney" and "Alligator Pie" from ALLIGATOR PIE by Dennis Lee. Copyright © 1974 by Dennis Lee. Canadian rights administered by Macmillan of Canada, a Division of Gage Publishing Limited. "The Muddy Puddle" from GARBAGE DELIGHT by Dennis Lee. Copyright © 1977 by Dennis Lee. Canadian rights administered by Macmillan of Canada, a Division of Gage Publishing Limited. "Sea Shell" from THE COMPLETE POETICAL WORKS OF AMY LOWELL. Copyright 1955 by Houghton Mifflin Company. "Oliphaunt" from THE ADVENTURES OF TOM BOMBADIL by J. R. R. Tolkien. Copyright © 1962 by George Allen & Unwin Ltd. Canadian rights administered by George Allen & Unwin Ltd. Reprinted by permission of Houghton Mifflin Company.

Barbara A. Huff for "The Library." Copyright © by Barbara A. Huff.

Olwyn Hughes for "Roger the Dog" from A FIRST POETRY BOOK by Ted Hughes. Published by Oxford University Press.

Instructor Publications, Inc., for "A Football Game" by Alice Van Eck, reprinted from *Instructor*, November 1960. Copyright © 1960 by The F. A. Owen Publishing Company. "Holding Hands" by Lenore Link, reprinted from *St. Nicholas Magazine*, June 1936. Published by Macmillan in 1937 in UNDER THE TENT OF THE SKY, John E. Brewton, editor. Reprint rights now controlled by The Instructor Publications, Inc. Copyright by The Instructor Publications, Inc. Reprinted by permission.

International Creative Management for "Mark's Fingers" from FINGERS ARE ALWAYS BRINGING ME NEWS by Mary O'Neill. Copyright © 1969 by Mary O'Neill. Published by Doubleday & Company, Inc.

Robert C. Jackson for "Grandpa Dropped His Glasses" and "Beela by the Sea" by Leroy F. Jackson.

Barbara Boyden Jordan for "Mud" by Polly Chase Boyden.

Michael Joseph Ltd. for "The Ants at the Olympics" and "The Duck" from ANIMAL ALPHABET by Richard Digance. Published by Michael Joseph Ltd.

May Justus for "Jessica Jane" and "The Rain Has Silver Sandals." Reprinted by permission of the author and Abingdon Press.

Kansas City Star Company for "The Winning of the TV West" by John T. Alexander.

Bobbi Katz for "Patience," copyright © 1979. "The Runaway," copyright © 1981. "Samuel," copyright © 1972. "Spring Is," copyright © 1979. "Things to Do If You Are a Subway," copyright © 1970.

Sidney B. Kramer for "Song" from THE CANTILEVER RAINBOW by Ruth Krauss. Copyright © 1965, 1976 by Ruth Krauss.

B. J. Lee for "Eight Witches" by B. J. Lee (pseudonym for Leland B. Jacobs) from ARITHMETIC IN VERSE AND RHYME, Allan D. Jacobs and Leland B. Jacobs, editors. Copyright © 1971 by Leland B. Jacobs. Published by Garrard Publishing Co.

Dennis Lee for "Double-Barreled Ding-Dong-Bat" and "Freddy" by Dennis Lee from BREAKFAST, BOOKS & DREAMS, Michael Patrick Hearn, editor. Copyright © 1981 by Dennis Lee. Published by Frederick Warne.

Little, Brown and Company for "The Waltzer in the House" from THE POEMS OF STANLEY KUNITZ 1928–1978. Copyright © 1958 by Stanley Kunitz. "Mr. Bidery's Spidery Garden" and "Every Time I Climb a Tree" from ONE AT A TIME: HIS COLLECTED POEMS FOR THE YOUNG by David McCord. Copyright © 1952, 1970 by David McCord. "Yellow" and #8 from "A Christmas Package: Nine Poems" from AWAY AND AGO: RHYMES OF THE NEVER WAS AND ALWAYS IS by David McCord. Copyright © 1968, 1974 by David McCord. "To Walk in Warm Rain" from SPEAK UP: MORE RHYMES OF THE NEVER WAS AND ALWAYS IS by David McCord. Copyright © 1979, 1980 by David McCord. "Adventures of Isabel" from THE BAD PARENTS' GARDEN OF VERSE by Ogden Nash. Copyright 1936 by Ogden Nash. "The People Upstairs," copyright 1949 by Ogden Nash. "The Cow," copyright 1931 by Ogden Nash. First appeared in *The Saturday Evening Post*. "Celery," copyright 1941 by The Curtis Publishing Company. First appeared in *The Saturday Evening Post*. "The Canary," copyright 1940 by The Curtis Publishing Company. First appeared in *The Saturday Evening Post*. "The Wendigo," copyright 1953 by Ogden Nash. "The Pizza," copyright © 1957 by Ogden Nash. All from VERSES FROM 1929 ON by Ogden Nash. "Eletelephony" from TIRRA LIRRA: RHYMES OLD AND NEW by Laura E. Richards. Copyright 1932 by Laura E. Richards, renewed 1960 by Hamilton Richards. Reprinted by permission of Little, Brown and Company.

Liveright Publishing Corporation for "hist whist" from TULIPS AND CHIMNEYS by e. e. cummings. Reprinted by permission of Liveright Publishing Corporation. Copyright 1923, 1925 by e. e. cummings, renewed 1951, 1953 by e. e. cummings. Copyright © 1973, 1976 by Nancy T. Andrews. Copyright © 1973, 1976 by George James Firmage.

Barbara Kunz Loots for "Mountain Wind."

McGraw-Hill Book Company for "Maple Feast" and "The Sandpiper" from THE LITTLE WHISTLER by Frances Frost. Copyright 1949 by McGraw-Hill Book Company. "Night Heron" from THE LITTLE NATURALIST by Frances Frost. Copyright © 1959 by Frances Frost and Kurt Werth. Reprinted by permission of McGraw-Hill Book Company.

McIntosh and Otis, Inc., for "Rhinos Purple, Hippos Green" from BREAKFAST, BOOKS & DREAMS by Michael Patrick Hearn. Copyright © 1981 by Michael Patrick Hearn. Published by Frederick Warne. "Fishes' Evening Song" from WHISPERING AND OTHER THINGS by Dahlov Ipcar. Copyright © 1967 by Dahlov Ipcar. Published by Alfred A. Knopf, Inc. Reprinted by permission of McIntosh and Otis, Inc.

Gail Kredenser Mack for "Polar Bear" and "Brontosaurus" from THE ABC OF BUMPTIOUS BEASTS by Gail Kredenser. Copyright © 1966 by Gail Kredenser. Published by Harlin Quist.

Macmillan Accounts and Administration Ltd. for "Camel" from BROWN JOHN'S BEASTS by Alan Brownjohn. Reprinted by permission of Macmillan, London and Basingstoke (The Macmillan Company of Canada Ltd.).

Macmillan Publishing Co., Inc., for "Mountain Brook" from SUMMER GREEN by Elizabeth Coatsworth. Copyright 1948 by Macmillan Publishing Co., Inc., renewed 1976 by Elizabeth Coatsworth Beston. "Sea Gull" from SUMMER GREEN by Elizabeth Coatsworth. Copyright 1947 by Macmillan Publishing Co., Inc., renewed 1975 by Elizabeth Coatsworth Beston. "Something Told the Wild Geese" and "The Performing Seal" from BRANCHES GREEN by Rachel Field. Copyright 1934 by Macmillan Publishing Co., Inc., renewed 1962 by Arthur S. Pederson. "The Seven Ages of Elf-hood" from POEMS by Rachel Field. Copyright 1926 by Macmillan Publishing Co., Inc., renewed 1954 by Arthur S. Pederson. "City Lights" and "Some People" from POEMS by Rachel Field. Copyright © 1957 by Macmillan Publishing Co., Inc. "The Chipmunk's Song" from THE BAT-POET by Randall Jarrell. Copyright © 1963, 1964 by Macmillan Publishing Co., Inc. "The Moon's the North Wind's Cooky" from COLLECTED POEMS by Vachel Lindsay. Copyright 1914 by Macmillan Publishing Co., Inc., renewed 1942 by Elizabeth C. Lindsay. "Check" from COLLECTED POEMS by James Stephens. Copyright 1915 by Macmillan Publishing Co., Inc., renewed 1943 by James Stephens. "Little Things" from COLLECTED POEMS by James Stephens. Copyright 1926 by Macmillan Publishing Co., Inc., renewed 1954 by Cynthia Stephens. Canadian rights administered by Iris Wise and Macmillan, London and Basingstoke (The Macmillan Company of Canada, Ltd.). "February Twilight" from COLLECTED POEMS by Sara Teasdale. Copyright 1926 by Macmillan Publishing Co., Inc., renewed 1954 by Mamie T. Wheless. "To a Squirrel at Kyle-Na-No" from COLLECTED POEMS by William Butler Yeats. Copyright 1919 by Macmillan Publishing Co., Inc., renewed 1947 by Bertha Georgie Yeats. Canadian rights administered by A. P. Watt Ltd. Reprinted by permission of Macmillan Publishing Co., Inc.

Josephine Curry McNatt for "Smells" from POEMS FOR JOSEPHINE by Kathryn Worth.

Methuen, Inc., for "Grandpa Bear's Lullaby" from DRAGON NIGHT AND OTHER LULLABIES by Jane Yolen. Copyright © 1980 by Jane Yolen. Reprinted by permission of the publisher, Methuen, Inc.

James N. Miller for "Cat" by Mary Britton Miller.

John Travers Moore for "Going Up," copyright © 1983 by John Travers Moore, and "The Tree Frog," copyright © 1967 by John Travers Moore. Used by permission of the author.

Lillian Morrison for "Just for One Day." Original poem reprinted by permission of the author. "Air Traveler" by Lillian Morrison.

William Morrow & Company, Inc., for "My Mouth" and "Chocolate Chocolate" from EATS by Arnold Adoff. Copyright © 1979 by Arnold Adoff. Reprinted by permission of Lothrop, Lee & Shepard Books (A Division of William Morrow & Company, Inc.). "Summer" from COUNTRY PIE by Frank Asch. Copyright © 1979 by Frank Asch. "The Sugar Lady," "Sunrise," and "Alley Cat School" from CITY SANDWICH by Frank Asch. Copyright © 1978 by Frank Asch. "Oh the Toe Test!" from NEVER SAY UGH TO A BUG by Norma Farber. Copyright © 1979 by Norma Farber. Reprinted by permission of Greenwillow Books (A Division of William Morrow & Company, Inc.). "The Reason I Like Chocolate" from VACATION TIME by Nikki Giovanni. Copyright © 1980 by Nikki Giovanni. Reprinted by permission of William Morrow & Company, Inc. "Water's Edge" from WHO WOULD MARRY A MINERAL? by Lillian Morrison. Copyright © 1978 by Lillian Morrison. "The Knockout" and "On the Skateboard" from THE SIDEWALK RACER AND OTHER POEMS OF SPORTS AND ACTION by Lillian Morrison. Copyright © 1977 by Lillian Morrison. Reprinted by permission of Lothrop, Lee & Shepard Books (A Division of William Morrow & Company, Inc.). "The Darkling Elves" from THE HEADLESS HORSEMAN RIDES TONIGHT by Jack Prelutsky. Copyright © 1980 by Jack Prelutsky. "No Girls Allowed" from ROLLING HARVEY DOWN THE HILL by Jack Prelutsky. Copyright © 1980 by Jack Prelutsky. "Wrimples" from THE SNOPP ON THE SIDEWALK by Jack Prelutsky. Copyright © 1976, 1977 by Jack Prelutsky. "Pumberly Pott's Unpredictable Niece" and "Herbert Glerbett" from THE QUEEN OF EENE by Jack Prelutsky. Copyright © 1970, 1978 by Jack Prelutsky. "The Bogeyman" and "The Troll" from NIGHTMARES by Jack Prelutsky. Copyright © 1976 by Jack Prelutsky. "Long Gone" and "Don't Ever Seize a Weasel by the Tail," copyright © 1967, 1983 by Jack Prelutsky. Reprinted from ZOO DOINGS, copyright © 1983 by Jack Prelutsky. "The Hippopotamus," copyright © 1970, 1983 by Jack Prelutsky. Reprinted from ZOO DOINGS, copyright © 1983 by Jack Prelutsky. "The Lion" and "The Cow," copyright © 1974, 1983 by Jack Prelutsky. Reprinted from ZOO DOINGS, copyright © 1983 by Jack Prelutsky. Reprinted by permission of Greenwillow Books (A Division of William Morrow & Company, Inc.). "Crowds" and "Stickball" from SUBWAY SWINGER by Virginia Schonborg. Copyright © 1970 by Virginia Schonborg. Reprinted by permission of William Morrow & Company, Inc.

New Directions Publishing Corp. for "Johnnie Crack and Flossie Snail" from UNDER MILK WOOD by Dylan Thomas. Copyright 1954 by New Directions Publishing Corp. Canadian rights administered by David Higham Associates Limited. "This Is Just to Say" from COLLECTED EARLIER POEMS by William Carlos Williams. Copyright 1938 by New Directions Publishing Corp. Reprinted by permission of New Directions Publishing Corp.

The New Yorker Magazine, Inc., for "Hog-Calling Competition" by Morris Bishop. Copyright © 1936, 1964 by The New Yorker Magazine, Inc. "A Sad Song About Greenwich Village" by Frances Park. Copyright 1927, 1955 by The New Yorker Magazine, Inc.

Bonnie Nims for "How to Get There." Reprinted by permission of the author. J. Philip O'Hara, the publisher, is no longer in business.

Harold Ober Associates for "City" from THE LANGSTON HUGHES READER. Copyright © 1958 by Langston Hughes. Published by Braziller.

O. G. Phillips, Inc., for "I'm Alone in the Evening" from MIND YOUR OWN BUSINESS by Michael Rosen. Copyright © 1974 by Michael Rosen. Canadian rights administered by Andre Deutsch Ltd.

Plays, Inc., for "Wearing of the Green" from HOLIDAY PROGRAMS FOR BOYS AND GIRLS by Aileen Fisher. Copyright 1953 by Aileen Fisher. Plays, Inc., Publishers, Boston, MA.

Jack Prelutsky for "Nature Is," "The Four Seasons," "Dogs and Cats and Bears and Bats," "The Ways of Living Things," "City, Oh, City!," "Children, Children Everywhere," "ME I AM!," "Home! You're Where It's Warm Inside," "I'm Hungry!," "Some People I Know," "Nonsense! Nonsense!," "Alphabet Stew," "Where Goblins Dwell," and "The Land of Potpourri." Copyright © 1983 by Jack Prelutsky.

Prentice-Hall, Inc., for "Wanted—A Witch's Cat" from WHAT WITCHES DO by Shelagh McGee. Copyright © 1980 by Felix Gluck Press, Ltd. Published by Prentice-Hall, Inc., Englewood Cliffs, NJ 07632.

The Putnam Publishing Group for "My Nose," "When," and "When I Was Lost" from ALL TOGETHER by Dorothy Aldis. Copyright 1925–28, 1934, 1939, 1952 by Dorothy Aldis, renewed 1953–56, 1962, 1967. "Everybody Says" from HERE, THERE & EVERYWHERE by Dorothy Aldis. Copyright 1927, 1928 by Dorothy Aldis, renewed 1955, 1956. "Wasps" from IS ANYBODY HUNGRY? by Dorothy Aldis. Copyright © 1964 by Dorothy Aldis. Reprinted by permission of G. P. Putnam's Sons. "The Alligator" and "Gumble" from STUFF & NONSENSE by Michael Dugan. Copyright © 1974 by William Collins. "The Bluffalo" from HOW BEASTLY! by Jane Yolen. Copyright © 1980 by Jane Yolen. Reprinted by permission of Philomel Books, a Division of The Putnam Publishing Group.

Random House, Inc., for "Song of the Ogres" from W. H. AUDEN: COLLECTED POEMS, Edward Mendelson, editor. Copyright © 1968 by W. H. Auden. Reprinted by permission of Random House, Inc. "Ode to the Pig: His Tail," "Ode to Spring," "Thoughts on Talkers," and "Ants, Although Admirable, Are Awfully Aggravating" from THE COLLECTED POEMS OF FREDDY THE PIG by Walter R. Brooks. Copyright 1953 by Walter R. Brooks. "Aunt Sponge and Aunt Spiker" from JAMES AND THE GIANT PEACH by Roald Dahl. Copyright © 1961 by Roald Dahl. Reprinted by permission of Alfred A. Knopf, Inc. "Together" from EMBRACE: SELECTED LOVE POEMS by Paul Engle. Copyright © 1969 by Paul Engle. Reprinted by permission of Random House, Inc. "The Lizard" from A CHILD'S BESTIARY by John Gardner. Copyright © 1977 by Boskydell Artists, Ltd. "Winter Moon" from SELECTED POEMS OF LANGSTON HUGHES. Copyright 1926 by Alfred A. Knopf, Inc., renewed 1954 by Langston Hughes. "Dreams" and "April Rain Song" from THE DREAM KEEPER AND OTHER POEMS by Langston Hughes. Copyright 1932 by Alfred A. Knopf, Inc., renewed 1960 by Langston Hughes. Reprinted by permission of Alfred A. Knopf, Inc. "McIntosh Apple" from SLEEPY IDA AND OTHER NONSENSE POEMS by Steven Kroll. Copyright © 1977 by Steven Kroll. "Where Are You Now?" and "The Universe" from ALL ABOARD by Mary Britton Miller. Copyright © 1958 by Pantheon Books, Inc. "They've All Gone South" from LISTEN—THE BIRDS by Mary Britton Miller. Copyright © 1961 by Pantheon Books, Inc. "The Contrary Waiter" from STUFF & NONSENSE by Edgar Parker. Copyright © 1961 by Edgar Parker. Reprinted by permission of Pantheon Books, a Division of Random House, Inc. "Too Many Daves" from THE SNEETCHES AND OTHER STORIES by Dr. Seuss. Copyright © 1953, 1954, 1961 by Dr. Seuss. "If We Didn't Have Birthdays" from HAPPY BIRTHDAY TO YOU by Dr. Seuss. Copyright © 1959 by Dr. Seuss. Reprinted by permission of Random House, Inc. "January" and "August" from A CHILD'S CALENDAR by John Updike. Copyright © 1965 by John Updike and Nancy Burkert. Reprinted by permission of Alfred A. Knopf, Inc. "My Little Sister" from ALL ON A SUMMER'S DAY by William Wise. Copyright © 1971 by William Wise. Reprinted by permission of Pantheon Books, a Division of Random House, Inc.

Marian Reiner for "Lazy Witch" and "Mr. Pratt" from OLD MRS. TWINDLY-TART AND OTHER RHYMES. Copyright © 1967 by Myra Cohn Livingston.

Paul R. Reynolds, Inc., for "Eat-it-all Elaine," "Measles," and "Cockroaches" by Kaye Starbird. Copyright © 1963, 1966 by Kaye Starbird. Reprinted by permission of Paul R. Reynolds, Inc., 12 East 41st Street, New York, NY 10017.

Marci Ridlon for "My Brother" and "City, City" from THAT WAS SUMMER by Marci Ridlon. Copyright © 1969 by Marci Ridlon. Published by Follett Publishing Co. "Open Hydrant" and "Fernando" by Marci Ridlon.

Michael Rieu for "The Flattered Flying Fish," "The Lesser Lynx," "The Paint Box," "Sir Smasham Uppe," "Soliloquy of a Tortoise on Revisiting the Lettuce Beds After an Interval of One Hour While Supposed to Be Sleeping in a Clump of Blue Hollyhocks," and "Two People" by E. V. Rieu.

Lady Joan Roberts for "Ice" by Sir Charles Roberts.

St. Martin's Press, Inc., for "The Great Auk's Ghost" from COLLECTED POEMS by Ralph Hodgson. Copyright © 1961 by Ralph Hodgson. Canadian rights administered by George Allen & Unwin Ltd.

The Saturday Evening Post Company for "Far Trek" by June Brady. Copyright © 1974. "Hot Line" by Louella Dunann. Copyright © 1972 by The Curtis Publishing Company. Reprinted by permission from The Saturday Evening Post.

Susan Alton Schmeltz for "Paper Dragons," reprinted from *Cricket Magazine*, volume 6, number 7, March 1979. Copyright © 1979 by Susan M. Schmeltz.

Scholastic Inc. for "Wind-Wolves" by William D. Sargent. Copyright 1926 by Scholastic Inc. Reprinted by permission of Scholastic Inc. (Scholastic Writing Awards Program).

Frances Schwartz Literary Agency for the following poems by Arnold Spilka: "Don't Tell Me That I Talk Too Much!" from AND THE FROG "BLAH!" Copyright © 1972 by Arnold Spilka. "Flowers Are a Silly Bunch" from ONCE UPON A HORSE. Copyright © 1966 by Arnold Spilka. "I'm Really Not Lazy" and "I Saw a Little Girl I Hate" from A RUMBUDGIN. Copyright © 1970 by Arnold Spilka. "Puzzle" from A LION I CAN DO WITHOUT. Copyright © 1964 by Arnold Spilka.

Louise H. Sclove for "Habits of the Hippopotamus" and "Routine" from GAILY THE TROUBADOUR by Arthur Guiterman. "Harvest Home" from BRAVE LAUGHTER by Arthur Guiterman. "The Polliwog" by Arthur Guiterman. Reprinted by permission of Louise H. Sclove.

Charles Scribner's Sons for "Desert Tortoise" from DESERT VOICES by Byrd Baylor. Copyright © 1981 by Byrd Baylor (New York: Charles Scribner's Sons, 1981). "Ducks' Ditty" from THE WIND IN THE WILLOWS by Kenneth Grahame. Copyright 1908 by Charles Scribner's Sons (New York: Charles Scribner's Sons, 1908). "I Can Fly," "They're Calling," "Leave Me Alone," and "The City Dump" from AT THE TOP OF MY VOICE by Felice Holman. Copyright © 1970 by Felice Holman (New York: Charles Scribner's Sons, 1970). "Amelia Mixed the Mustard" by A. E. Housman from MY BROTHER, A. E. HOUSMAN by Laurence Housman. Copyright 1937, 1938 by Laurence Housman, copyrights renewed (New York: Charles Scribner's Sons, 1938). Reprinted by permission of Charles Scribner's Sons. Canadian rights administered by The Society of Authors.

R. C. Scriven for "The Marrog."

Ian Serraillier for "The Tickle Rhyme" from THE MONSTER HORSE. Copyright 1950 by Ian Serraillier. Published by Oxford University Press.

Richard Shaw for "Cat's Menu" by Winifred Crawford (aka Richard Shaw).

Sheed & Ward, Inc., for "Daddy Fell into the Pond" by Alfred Noyes. Copyright 1952 by Sheed & Ward, Inc. Reprinted by permission of Andrews and McMeel, Inc. All rights reserved.

Diane Siebert for "Train Song." Copyright © 1981 by Diane Siebert.

Simon & Schuster for "Slithergadee" from DON'T BUMP THE GLUMP! by Shel Silverstein. Copyright © 1964 by Shel Silverstein.

Norah Smaridge for "Why Run?" Copyright © by Norah Smaridge.

William Jay Smith for "Lion" from POEMS 1947–1957 by William Jay Smith. Copyright © 1957 by William Jay Smith. Published by Little, Brown and Company.

The Society of Authors for "Tired Tim," "Some One," "Silver," and "The Horseman" by Walter de la Mare. Reprinted by permission of the Literary Trustees of Walter de la Mare and The Society of Authors as their representative.

Jean Conder Soule for "Surprises."

Lloyd Sarett Stockdale for "Four Little Foxes" from COVENANT WITH EARTH: A SELECTION FROM THE POETRY OF LEW SARETT, Alma Johnson Sarett, editor. Copyright © 1956 by Alma Johnson Sarett (Gainesville: The University of Florida Press, 1956). "The Wolf Cry" from COLLECTED POEMS by Lew Sarett. Copyright © 1969 by Alma Johnson Sarett (Henry Holt and Company). Reprinted by permission of Lloyd Sarett Stockdale.

Margaret Winsor Stubbs for "This Little Pig Built a Spaceship" from THE SPACE CHILD'S MOTHER GOOSE.

Catherine R. Sullivan for "Measurement" from SELECTED LYRICS AND SONNETS by A. M. Sullivan. Copyright © 1970 by Catherine R. Sullivan (New York: Thomas Y. Crowell, 1970).

Dorothy Brown Thompson for "Maps," reprinted from *Target Magazine*. "Our House" and "This Is Halloween," reprinted from *Child Life Magazine*. Copyright reassigned to Dorothy Brown Thompson.

Viking Penguin Inc. for "Changing," "The Folk Who Live in Backward Town," "Meg's Egg," and "Waiters" from YELLOW BUTTER PURPLE JELLY RED JAM BLACK BREAD by Mary Ann Hoberman. Copyright © 1981 by Mary Ann Hoberman. "Clickbeetle" and "Praying Mantis" from BUGS by Mary Ann Hoberman. Copyright © 1976 by Mary Ann Hoberman. "Me" and "The Snowflake" from BELLS AND GRASS by Walter de la Mare. Copyright 1942 by Walter de la Mare, renewed 1969 by Richard de la Mare. "The People" and "The Rabbit" from UNDER THE TREE by Elizabeth Madox Roberts. Copyright 1922 by B. W. Huebsch, renewed 1950 by Ivor S. Roberts. "Joyful" from FROM SUMMER TO SUMMER by Rose Burgunder Styron. Copyright © 1965 by Rose Styron. Reprinted by permission of Viking Penguin Inc.

Walker and Company for "Colonel Fazackerley" from FIGGIE HOBBIN by Charles Causley. Copyright © 1973 by Charles Causley.

Watson-Guptill Publications for "Advice to Small Children" and "Let Others Share" from EVERY DOG HAS HIS SAY by Edward Anthony. Copyright 1947, © 1975 by Watson-Guptill Publications. Reprinted by permission of Watson-Guptill Publications.

A. P. Watt Ltd. for "The Pumpkin" from COLLECTED POEMS by Robert Graves. Reprinted by permission of Robert Graves.

Mabel Watts for "Maytime Magic," reprinted from *Humpty Dumpty Magazine*, 1954. "The Riveter" by Mabel Watts. Reprinted by permission of Mabel Watts.

Wesleyan University Press for "The Base Stealer" from THE ORB WEAVER by Robert Francis. Copyright © 1960 by Robert Francis. Reprinted by permission of Wesleyan University Press. This poem first appeared in *Forum*.

James T. White & Co. for "Birch Trees" by John Richard Moreland.

Xerox Education Publications for "Foul Shot" by Edwin A. Hoey, reprinted from *Read Magazine*. Copyright © 1962 by Xerox Education Publications. Reprinted by permission of *Read Magazine*.

Adam Yarmolinsky for "A Pig Is Never Blamed" by Babette Deutsch.

Additional acknowledgments:

Atheneum Publishers, Inc., for "In the Motel" from THE PHANTOM ICE CREAM MAN: MORE NONSENSE VERSE by X. J. Kennedy. Copyright © 1979 by X. J. Kennedy. A Margaret K. McElderry Book (New York: Atheneum, 1979). "Mother's Nerves," "Father and Mother," and "Help!" from ONE WINTER IN AUGUST AND OTHER NONSENSE JINGLES by X. J. Kennedy. Copyright © 1975 by X. J. Kennedy. A Margaret K. McElderry Book (New York: Atheneum, 1975). Reprinted by permission of Atheneum Publishers, Inc.

Gretchen Van Meter for "Leopard." Copyright © 1977 by Gretchen Van Meter. "Leopard" first appeared in *Cricket*, January 1978, vol. 5, no. 5. "I'm Nobody! Who Are You?" reprinted by permission of the publishers and the Trustees of Amherst College from THE POEMS OF EMILY DICKINSON edited by Thomas H. Johnson, Cambridge, Mass.: The Belknap Press of Harvard University Press, Copyright 1951, © 1955, 1979, 1983 by the President and Fellows of Harvard College.

CONTENTS

Dogs and Cats and Bears and Bats   52

The Ways of Living Things   71

Me I Am!   117

Home! You're Where It's Warm Inside   131

14

INTRODUCTION

FOR VERY YOUNG CHILDREN, responding to poetry is as natural as breathing. Even before they can speak, most babies delight in the playful cadences of nursery rhymes and the soothing rhythms of lullabies. For the toddler, Mother Goose favorites are an integral part of life. Poetry is as delightful and surprising as being tickled or catching a snowflake on a mitten. Young children are fascinated by the visual images of "The Old Woman Who Lived in a Shoe." They revel in the rhythms of "Peter, Peter, Pumpkin Eater." And although they may not quite understand the meaning, they are enchanted by the wordplay of "Sing a Song of Sixpence."

But then something happens to this early love affair with poetry. At some point during their school careers, many children seem to lose their interest and enthusiasm for poetry and their easygoing pleasure in its sounds and images. They begin to find poetry boring and irrelevant, too difficult or too dull to bother with.

For the last few years I've been visiting schools, colleges, and libraries throughout the United States and Canada, working directly with children. In reading and reciting poetry to them, I've begun to understand the kinds of poems to which children respond—poems that evoke laughter and delight, poems that cause a palpable ripple of surprise by the unexpected comparisons they make, poems that paint pictures with words that are as vivid as brushstrokes, poems that reawaken pleasure in the sounds and meanings of language. Repeated requests from teachers and librarians to recommend a comprehensive anthology of such poems provided the impetus for *The Random House Book of Poetry for Children*.

When I assembled this collection, I decided to focus on poems for elementary school children—the kids I know best. I felt that this group provided a sufficiently wide age range, although there are undoubtedly many poems in the collection that will appeal to preschoolers and others that will please adolescents. There are, however, no nursery rhymes, which my target audience might find babyish; nor are there poems that specifically cater to such adolescent concerns as romantic love (and acne). Parents and teachers of preschoolers, therefore, should be selective in using the book. A poem that might be deliciously scary for an eight-year-old might be terrifying to a four-year-old. My criteria for selecting poems were rhythm, rhyme, and imagery that did not sacrifice clarity of meaning. I looked for poems that deal with topics of interest to children in a way that delights the ear. I have avoided many of the "inspirational" and the long narrative poems that are so often included in other anthologies because they no longer seem relevant to today's children, morally uplifting though they may have been to earlier generations. On the other hand, I have included such writers as Lewis

Carroll and A. A. Milne because their magic with words withstands the test of time. While most of the poets represented are primarily children's poets, there are some poems by poets who are generally considered "adult" poets, such as Robert Frost, Christopher Morley, and John Updike. Sometimes these poets wrote an occasional poem for children; other times their poetry has a beautiful simplicity that makes it appealing and meaningful to both children and adults. Quite frankly, I tried to fill this book with poems I believe *elementary school children* will like. While there are many poignant and serious poems in the collection, the accent is on humor and light verse.

During the last thirty or forty years there has been a renaissance in children's poetry. Many of the best children's poets who ever wrote are writing today. Such contemporary writers as Aileen Fisher, John Ciardi, Lilian Moore, Dennis Lee, and Shel Silverstein, to name a handful, are creating children's poetry that is relevant, understandable, and thoroughly enjoyable. Such poets, unlike some of their pedantic predecessors, do not set out to educate children in a way that will make them more socially acceptable to adult company. They write from the child within themselves for "other" children, using the technical skills and insights of mature artists. Not unlike artists who create work for adults, they shape the way reality is perceived. They enrich daily experience. Who can see a field of blazing sunflowers and not remember them as Van Gogh painted them? Try reading Lilian Moore's "Until I Saw the Sea," for example, before your next excursion to the beach. Then you, too, will see the sea breathe "in and out" when you watch the surf. After reading John Ciardi's "Mummy Slept Late and Daddy Fixed Breakfast," when some child receives a waffle that looks "like a manhole cover," the experience will have a universality, a special element of humor, that it would not have had without the child's experiencing the poem. Unlike the poems in many other "comprehensive" anthologies, two thirds of the poems in this collection were first published during the past four decades.

As the table of contents shows, I have divided the anthology into fourteen broad sections. In addition to the table of contents and the usual indexes of author, title, and first line, I have included a subject index. I hope that it will prove valuable, especially to teachers, who can use it to add the fun and beauty of poetry to subjects in the school curriculum and to events during the year.

I am especially delighted that Arnold Lobel, a Caldecott Award winner, agreed to illustrate the collection. It is difficult to imagine a child looking at these illustrations and not wanting to read the poems! I hope that our combined efforts will introduce children everywhere to many new, wonderful, and unexpected ways of looking at the world.

JACK PRELUTSKY

Albuquerque, New Mexico
April 1983

NATURE IS

Nature is the endless sky,
the sun of golden light,
a cloud that floats serenely by,
the silver moon of night.

Nature is a sandy dune,
a tall and stately tree,
the waters of a clear lagoon,
the billows on the sea.

Nature is a gentle rain
and winds that howl and blow,
a thunderstorm, a hurricane,
a silent field of snow.

Nature is a tranquil breeze
and pebbles on a shore.
Nature's each and all of these
and infinitely more.

Auguries of Innocence

To see a World in a grain of sand,
And a Heaven in a wild flower,
Hold Infinity in the palm of your hand,
And Eternity in an hour.

William Blake

I'm Glad the Sky Is Painted Blue

I'm glad the sky is painted blue,
    And the earth is painted green,
With such a lot of nice fresh air
    All sandwiched in between.

Anonymous

The Universe

There is the moon, there is the sun
Round which we circle every year,
And there are all the stars we see
On starry nights when skies are clear,
And all the countless stars that lie
Beyond the reach of human eye.
If every bud on every tree,
All birds and fireflies and bees
And all the flowers that bloom and die
Upon the earth were counted up,
The number of the stars would be
Greater, they say, than all of these.

Mary Britton Miller

All Things Bright and Beautiful

All things bright and beautiful,
    All creatures great and small,
All things wise and wonderful,
    The Lord God made them all.

Each little flower that opens,
    Each little bird that sings,
He made their glowing colors,
    He made their tiny wings.

The purple-headed mountain,
    The river running by,
The sunset, and the morning,
    That brightens up the sky;

The cold wind in the winter,
    The pleasant summer sun,
The ripe fruits in the garden,
    He made them every one.

He gave us eyes to see them,
    And lips that we might tell,
How great is God Almighty,
    Who has made all things well.

Cecil Frances Alexander

On the Bridge

If I could see a little fish—
That is what I just now wish!
I want to see his great round eyes
Always open in surprise.

I wish a water-rat would glide
Slowly to the other side;
Or a dancing spider sit
On the yellow flags a bit.

I think I'll get some stones to throw,
And watch the pretty circles show.
Or shall we sail a flower-boat,
And watch it slowly—slowly float?

That's nice—because you never know
How far away it means to go;
And when tomorrow comes, you see,
It may be in the great wide sea.

Kate Greenaway

Flint

An emerald is as green as grass,
    A ruby red as blood;
A sapphire shines as blue as heaven;
    A flint lies in the mud.

A diamond is a brilliant stone,
    To catch the world's desire;
An opal holds a fiery spark;
    But a flint holds fire.

Christina Rossetti

Measurement

Stars and atoms have no size,
They only vary in men's eyes.

Men and instruments will blunder
Calculating things of wonder.

A seed is just as huge a world
As any ball the sun has hurled.

Stars are quite as picayune
As any splinter of the moon.

Time is but a vague device;
Space can never be precise;

Stars and atoms have a girth,
Small as zero, ten times Earth.

There is, by God's swift reckoning
A universe in everything.

A. M. Sullivan

The Secret Song

Who saw the petals
   drop from the rose?
I, said the spider,
But nobody knows.

Who saw the sunset
   flash on a bird?
I, said the fish,
But nobody heard.

Who saw the fog
   come over the sea?
I, said the sea pigeon,
Only me.

Who saw the first
   green light of the sun?
I, said the night owl,
The only one.

Who saw the moss
   creep over the stone?
I, said the gray fox,
All alone.

Margaret Wise Brown

The Wolf Cry

The Arctic moon hangs overhead;
The wide white silence lies below.
A starveling pine stands lone and gaunt,
Black-penciled on the snow.

Weird as the moan of sobbing winds,
A lone long call floats up from the trail;
And the naked soul of the frozen North
Trembles in that wail.

Lew Sarett

Last Rites

Dead in the cold, a song-singing thrush,
Dead at the foot of a snowberry bush—
Weave him a coffin of rush,
Dig him a grave where the soft mosses grow,
Raise him a tombstone of snow.

Christina Rossetti

Trees

The Oak is called the king of trees,
The Aspen quivers in the breeze,
The Poplar grows up straight and tall,
The Peach tree spreads along the wall,
The Sycamore gives pleasant shade,
The Willow droops in watery glade,
The Fir tree useful timber gives,
The Beech amid the forest lives.

Sara Coleridge

The Crocus

The golden crocus reaches up
To catch a sunbeam in her cup.

Walter Crane

Dandelion

O little soldier with the golden helmet,
What are you guarding on my lawn?
You with your green gun
And your yellow beard,
Why do you stand so stiff?
There is only the grass to fight!

Hilda Conkling

Birch Trees

The night is white,
   The moon is high,
The birch trees lean
   Against the sky.

The cruel winds
   Have blown away
Each little leaf
   Of silver gray.

O lonely trees
   As white as wool . . .
That moonlight makes
   So beautiful.

John Richard Moreland

The Ferns

High, high in the branches
the seawinds plunge and roar.
A storm is moving westward,
but here on the forest floor
the ferns have captured stillness.
A green sea growth they are.

The ferns lie underwater
in a light of the forest's green.
Their motion is like stillness,
as if water shifts between
and a great storm quivers
through fathoms of green.

Gene Baro

Wind-Wolves

Do you hear the cry as the pack goes by,
The wind-wolves hunting across the sky?
Hear them tongue it, keen and clear,
Hot on the flanks of the flying deer!

Across the forest, mere, and plain,
Their hunting howl goes up again!
All night they'll follow the ghostly trail,
All night we'll hear their phantom wail,

For tonight the wind-wolf pack holds sway
From Pegasus Square to the Milky Way,
And the frightened bands of cloud-deer flee
In scattered groups of two and three.

William D. Sargent

Mountain Wind

Windrush down the timber chutes
   between the mountain's knees—
     a hiss of distant breathing,
      a shouting in the trees,
       a recklessness of branches,
        a wilderness a-sway,
         when suddenly
a silence
takes your breath away.

Barbara Kunz Loots

The Wind

I can get through a doorway without any key,
And strip the leaves from the great oak tree.

I can drive storm-clouds and shake tall towers,
Or steal through a garden and not wake the flowers.

Seas I can move and ships I can sink;
I can carry a house-top or the scent of a pink.

When I am angry I can rave and riot;
And when I am spent, I lie quiet as quiet.

James Reeves

Windy Nights

Whenever the moon and stars are set,
Whenever the wind is high,
All night long in the dark and wet,
   A man goes riding by.
Late in the night when the fires are out,
Why does he gallop and gallop about?

Whenever the trees are crying aloud,
   And ships are tossed at sea,
By, on the highway, low and loud,
   By at the gallop goes he;
By at the gallop he goes, and then
By he comes back at the gallop again.

Robert Louis Stevenson

Who Has Seen the Wind?

Who has seen the wind?
   Neither I nor you:
But when the leaves hang trembling,
   The wind is passing through.

Who has seen the wind?
   Neither you nor I:
But when the leaves bow down their heads,
   The wind is passing by.

Christina Rossetti

Mountain Brook

Because of the steepness,
the streamlet runs white,
narrow and broken
as lightning by night.

Because of the rocks,
it leaps this way and that,
fresh as a flower,
quick as a cat.

Elizabeth Coatsworth

River Winding

Rain falling, what things do you grow?
Snow melting, where do you go?
Wind blowing, what trees do you know?
River winding, where do you flow?

Charlotte Zolotow

Mud

Mud is very nice to feel
All squishy-squash between the toes!
I'd rather wade in wiggly mud
Than smell a yellow rose.

Nobody else but the rosebush knows
How nice mud feels
Between the toes.

Polly Chase Boyden

The Muddy Puddle

I am sitting
In the middle
Of a rather Muddy
Puddle,
With my bottom
Full of bubbles
And my rubbers
Full of Mud,

While my jacket
And my sweater
Go on slowly
Getting wetter
As I very
Slowly settle
To the Bottom
Of the Mud.

And I find that
What a person
With a puddle
Round his middle
Thinks of mostly
In the muddle
Is the Muddi-
Ness of Mud.

Dennis Lee

Water's Edge

Wave swashes
foam splashes
ripple swishes
backwashes
dead fishes
and pools
with little live ones
deliciously
going about their business.

Lillian Morrison

Sea Shell

Sea Shell, Sea Shell,
Sing me a song, O please!
A song of ships, and sailor men,
And parrots, and tropical trees,

Of islands lost in the Spanish Main
Which no man ever may find again,
Of fishes and corals under the waves,
And sea horses stabled in great green caves.

Sea Shell, Sea Shell,
Sing of the things you know so well.

Amy Lowell

The Sea

Behold the wonders of the mighty deep,
Where crabs and lobsters learn to creep,
And little fishes learn to swim,
And clumsy sailors tumble in.

Anonymous

The Rain Has Silver Sandals

The rain has silver sandals
  For dancing in the spring,
And shoes with golden tassels
  For summer's frolicking.
Her winter boots have hobnails
  Of ice from heel to toe,
Which now and then she changes
  For moccasins of snow.

May Justus

Until I Saw the Sea

Until I saw the sea
I did not know
that wind
could wrinkle water so.

I never knew
that sun
could splinter a whole sea of blue.

Nor
did I know before,
a sea breathes in and out
upon a shore.

Lilian Moore

The More It Snows

The more it
SNOWS-tiddely-pom,
The more it
GOES-tiddely-pom
The more it
GOES-tiddely-pom
On
Snowing.

And nobody
KNOWS-tiddely-pom,
How cold my
TOES-tiddely-pom
How cold my
TOES-tiddely-pom
Are
Growing.

A. A. Milne

Rhyme

I like to see a thunder storm,
    A dunder storm,
        A blunder storm,
I like to see it, black and slow,
Come stumbling down the hills.

I like to hear a thunder storm,
    A plunder storm,
        A wonder storm,
Roar loudly at our little house
And shake the window sills!

Elizabeth Coatsworth

Rain Clouds

Along a road
Not built by man
There winds a silent
Caravan
Of camel-clouds
Whose humped gray backs
Are weighted down
With heavy packs
Of long-awaited,
Precious rain
To make the old earth
Young again,
And dress her shabby
Fields and hills
In green grass silk
With wild-flower frills.

Elizabeth-Ellen Long

To Walk in Warm Rain

To walk in warm rain
    And get wetter and wetter!
To do it again—
To walk in warm rain
    Till you drip like a drain.
To walk in warm rain
    And get wetter and wetter.

David McCord

When All the World Is Full of Snow

I never know
just where to go,
when all the world
is full of snow.

I do not want
to make a track,
not even
to the shed and back.

I only want
to watch and wait,
while snow moths settle
on the gate,

and swarming frost flakes
fill the trees
with billions
of albino bees.

I only want
myself to be
as silent as
a winter tree,

to hear the swirling
stillness grow,
when all the world
is full of snow.

N. M. Bodecker

First Snow

Snow makes whiteness where it falls.
The bushes look like popcorn-balls.
And places where I always play,
Look like somewhere else today.

Marie Louise Allen

Stopping by Woods on a Snowy Evening

Whose woods these are I think I know.
His house is in the village though;
He will not see me stopping here
To watch his woods fill up with snow.

My little horse must think it queer
To stop without a farmhouse near
Between the woods and frozen lake
The darkest evening of the year.

He gives his harness bells a shake
To ask if there is some mistake.
The only other sound's the sweep
Of easy wind and downy flake.

The woods are lovely, dark and deep,
But I have promises to keep,
And miles to go before I sleep.
And miles to go before I sleep.

Robert Frost

Check

The Night was creeping on the ground!
She crept, and did not make a sound

Until she reached the tree: And then
She covered it, and stole again

Along the grass beside the wall!
—I heard the rustling of her shawl

As she threw blackness everywhere
Along the sky, the ground, the air,

And in the room where I was hid!
But, no matter what she did

To everything that was without,
She could not put my candle out!

So I stared at the Night! And she
Stared back solemnly at me!

James Stephens

The Snowflake

Before I melt,
Come, look at me!
This lovely icy filigree!
Of a great forest
In one night
I make a wilderness
Of white:
By skyey cold
Of crystals made,
All softly, on
Your finger laid,
I pause, that you
My beauty see:
Breathe, and I vanish
Instantly.

Walter de la Mare

The Moon's the North Wind's Cook

The Moon's the North Wind's cooky.
He bites it, day by day,
Until there's but a rim of scraps
That crumble all away.

The South Wind is a baker.
He kneads clouds in his den,
And bakes a crisp new moon that . . . *greed*
North . . . Wind . . . eats . . . again!

Vachel Lindsay

Night Comes . . .

Night comes
leaking
out of the sky.

Stars come
peeking.

Moon comes
sneaking,
silvery-sly.

Who is
shaking,
shivery-
quaking?

Who is afraid
of the night?

Not I.

Beatrice Schenk de Regniers

Night

The night is coming softly, slowly;
Look, it's getting hard to see.
    Through the windows,
    Through the door,
    Pussyfooting
    On the floor,
    Dragging shadows,
    Crawling,
    Creeping,
    Soon it will be time for sleeping.
Pull down the shades.
Turn on the light.
Let's pretend it isn't night.

Mary Ann Hoberman

The Star

Twinkle, twinkle, little star,
How I wonder what you are!
Up above the world so high,
Like a diamond in the sky.

As your bright and tiny spark,
Lights the traveler in the dark—
Though I know not what you are,
Twinkle, twinkle, little star.

Jane Taylor

Silver

Slowly, silently, now the moon
Walks the night in her silver shoon;
This way, and that, she peers, and sees
Silver fruit upon silver trees;
One by one the casements catch
Her beams beneath the silvery thatch;
Couched in his kennel, like a log,
With paws of silver sleeps the dog;
From their shadowy cote the white breasts peep
Of doves in a silver-feathered sleep;
A harvest mouse goes scampering by,
With silver claws, and silver eye;
And moveless fish in the water gleam,
By silver reeds in a silver stream.

Walter de la Mare

The Night Is a Big Black Cat

The Night is a big black cat
    The Moon is her topaz eye,
The stars are the mice she hunts at night,
    In the field of the sultry sky.

G. Orr Clark

THE FOUR SEASONS

Summer
The earth is warm, the sun's ablaze,
it is a time of carefree days;
and bees abuzz that chance to pass
may see me snoozing on the grass.

Fall
The leaves are yellow, red, and brown,
a shower sprinkles softly down;
the air is fragrant, crisp, and cool,
and once again I'm stuck in school.

Winter
The birds are gone, the world is white,
the winds are wild, they chill and bite;
the ground is thick with slush and sleet,
and I can barely feel my feet.

Spring
The fields are rich with daffodils,
a coat of clover cloaks the hills,
and I must dance, and I must sing
to see the beauty of the spring.

36

Four Seasons

Spring is showery, flowery, bower
Summer: hoppy, choppy, poppy.
Autumn: wheezy, sneezy, freezy.
Winter: slippy, drippy, nippy.

Anonymous

The Months

January brings the snow,
Makes our feet and fingers glow.

February brings the rain,
Thaws the frozen lake again.

March brings breezes loud and shrill,
Stirs the dancing daffodil.

April brings the primrose sweet,
Scatters daisies at our feet.

May brings flocks of pretty lambs,
Skipping by their fleecy dams.

June brings tulips, lilies, roses,
Fills the children's hands with posies.

Hot July brings cooling showers,
Apricots and gillyflowers.

August brings the sheaves of corn,
Then the harvest home is borne.

Warm September brings the fruit,
Sportsmen then begin to shoot.

Fresh October brings the pheasant,
Then to gather nuts is pleasant.

Dull November brings the blast,
Then the leaves are whirling fast.

Chill December brings the sleet,
Blazing fire, and Christmas treat.

Sara Coleridge

January

The days are short,
    The sun a spark
Hung thin between
    The dark and dark

Fat snowy footsteps
    Track the floor.
Milk bottles burst
    Outside the door.

The river is
    A frozen place
Held still beneath
    The trees of lace.

The sky is low.
    The wind is gray.
The radiator
    Purrs all day.

John Updike

Lincoln

There was a boy of other days,
A quiet, awkward, earnest lad,
Who trudged long weary miles to get
A book on which his heart was set—
And then no candle had!

He was too poor to buy a lamp
But very wise in woodmen's ways.
He gathered seasoned bough and stem,
And crisping leaf, and kindled them
Into a ruddy blaze.

Then as he lay full length and read,
The firelight flickered on his face,
And etched his shadow on the gloom,
And made a picture in the room,
In that most humble place.

The hard years came, the hard years went,
But, gentle, brave, and strong of will,
He met them all. And when today
We see his pictured face, we say,
"There's light upon it still."

Nancy Byrd Turner

Martin Luther King

Got me a special place
For Martin Luther King.
His picture on the wall
Makes me sing.

I look at it for a long time
And think of some
Real good ways
We will overcome.

Myra Cohn Livingston

Ground Hog Day

Ground Hog sleeps
All winter
Snug in his fur,
Dreams
Green dreams of
Grassy shoots,
Of nicely newly nibbly
Roots—
Ah, he starts to
Stir.
With drowsy
Stare
Looks from his burrow
Out on fields of
Snow.
What's there?
Oh no.
His shadow. Oh,
How sad!
Six more
Wintry
Weeks
To go.

Lilian Moore

Beyond Winter

Over the winter glaciers
    I see the summer glow,
And through the wild-piled snowdrift
    The warm rosebuds below.

Ralph Waldo Emerson

Ice

When Winter scourged the meadow and the hill
And in the withered leafage worked his will,
The water shrank, and shuddered, and stood sti[ll]
Then built himself a magic house of glass,
Irised with memories of flowers and grass,
Wherein to sit and watch the fury pass.

Charles G. D. Rober[ts]

Valentine

I got a valentine from   Timmy
    Jimmy
    Tillie
    Billie
    Nicky
    Micky
    Ricky
    Dicky
    Laura
    Nora
    Cora
    Flora
    Donnie
    Ronnie
    Lonnie
    Connie
Eva even sent me two
But I didn't get *none* from you.

Shel Silverstein

Smells

Through all the frozen winter
My nose has grown most lonely
For lovely, lovely, colored smells
That come in springtime only.

The purple smell of lilacs,
The yellow smell that blows
Across the air of meadows
Where bright forsythia grows.

The tall pink smell of peach trees,
The low white smell of clover,
And everywhere the great green smell
Of grass the whole world over.

Kathryn Worth

Washington

He played by the river when he was young,
He raced with rabbits along the hills,
He fished for minnows, and climbed and swung,
And hooted back at the whippoorwills.
Strong and slender and tall he grew—
And then, one morning, the bugles blew.

Over the hills the summons came,
Over the river's shining rim.
He said that the bugles called his name,
He knew that his country needed him,
And he answered, "Coming!" and marched away
For many a night and many a day.

Perhaps when the marches were hot and long
He'd think of the river flowing by
Or, camping under the winter sky,
Would hear the whippoorwill's far-off song.
Boy or soldier, in peace or strife,
He loved America all his life!

Nancy Byrd Turner

February Twilight

I stood beside a hill
 Smooth with new-laid snow,
A single star looked out
 From the cold evening glow.

There was no other creature
 That saw what I could see—
I stood and watched the evening star
 As long as it watched me.

Sara Teasdale

Paper Dragons

In March, kites bite the wind
and shake their paper scales.
They strain against their fiber chains
to free their dragon tails.

Susan Alton Schmeltz

Maple Feast

Into the bit-flaked sugar-snow
The crystal-gathering sledges go.

Stumbling through silver to my knees,
I shout among the maple trees,

Tilt gleaming buckets icy cold
Till I am full as I can hold

Of clear bright sap, until I feel
Like a maple tree from head to heel!

Then to the sugarhouse I run
Where syrup, golden as the sun,

Is boiling in the crisp March air
And I, as daft as a baby bear,

Eat, till my buttons burst asunder
From maple sweetness, maple wonder!

Frances Frost

When

In February there are days,
Blue, and nearly warm,
When horses switch their tails and ducks
Go quacking through the farm.
When everything turns round to feel
The sun upon its back—
When winter lifts a little bit
And spring peeks through the crack.

Dorothy Aldis

March

A blue day,
a blue jay
and a good beginning.

One crow,
melting snow—
spring's winning!

Elizabeth Coatsworth

Wearing of the Green

It ought to come in April,
or, better yet, in May
when everything is green as green—
I mean St. Patrick's Day.

With still a week of winter
this wearing of the green
seems rather out of season—
it's rushing things, I mean.

But maybe March *is* better
when all is done and said:
St. Patrick brings a promise,
a four-leaf-clover promise,
a green-all-over promise
of springtime just ahead!

Aileen Fisher

The March Wind

I come to work as well as play;
    I'll tell you what I do;
I whistle all the live-long day,
    "Woo-oo-oo-oo! Woo-oo!"

I toss the branches up and down
    And shake them to and fro,
I whirl the leaves in flocks of brown,
    And send them high and low.

I strew the twigs upon the ground,
    The frozen earth I sweep;
I blow the children round and round
    And wake the flowers from sleep.

Anonymous

Daylight Saving Time

In Spring when maple buds are red,
We turn the Clock an hour ahead;
Which means, each April that arrives,
We lose an hour
Out of our lives.

Who cares? When Autumn birds in flocks
Fly southward, back we turn the Clocks,
And so regain a lovely thing—
That missing hour
We lost last Spring.

Phyllis McGinley

Easter

The air is like a butterfly
  With frail blue wings.
The happy earth looks at the sky
  And sings.

Joyce Kilmer

Spring Rain

The storm came up so very quick
  It couldn't have been quicker.
I should have brought my hat along,
  I should have brought my slicker.

My hair is wet, my feet are wet,
  I couldn't be much wetter.
I fell into a river once
  But this is even better.

Marchette Chute

Ode to Spring

O spring, O spring,
You wonderful thing!
O spring, O spring, O spring!
O spring, O spring,
When the birdies sing
I feel like a king,
  O spring!

Walter R. Brooks

Spring Is

Spring is when
    the morning sputters like
bacon
        and
          your
            sneakers
              run
                down
                  the
                    stairs
so fast you can hardly keep up with them,
and
spring is when
    your scrambled eggs
        jump
          off
            the
              plate
and turn into a million daffodils
trembling in the sunshine.

Bobbi Katz

Spring

I'm shouting
I'm singing
I'm swinging through trees
I'm winging sky-high
With the buzzing black bees.
I'm the sun
I'm the moon
I'm the dew on the rose.
I'm a rabbit
Whose habit
Is twitching his nose.
I'm lively
I'm lovely
I'm kicking my heels.
I'm crying "Come dance"
to the freshwater eels.
I'm racing through meadows
Without any coat
I'm a gamboling lamb
I'm a light leaping goat
I'm a bud
I'm a bloom
I'm a dove on the wing.
I'm running on rooftops
And welcoming spring!

Karla Kuskin

On Mother's Day

On Mother's Day we got up first,
so full of plans we almost burst.

We started breakfast right away
as our surprise for Mother's Day.

We picked some flowers, then hurried back
to make the coffee—rather black.

We wrapped our gifts and wrote a card
and boiled the eggs—a little hard.

And then we sang a serenade,
which burned the toast, I am afraid.

But Mother said, amidst our cheers,
"Oh, what a big surprise, my dears.
I've not had such a treat in years."
And she was smiling to her ears!

Aileen Fisher

Good-by My Winter Suit

Good-by my winter suit,
good-by my hat and boot,
good-by my ear-protecting muffs
and storms that hail and hoot.

Farewell to snow and sleet,
farewell to Cream of Wheat,
farewell to ice-removing salt
and slush around my feet.

Right on! to daffodils,
right on! to whippoorwills,
right on! to chirp-producing eggs
and baby birds and quills.

The day is on the wing,
the kite is on the string,
the sun is where the sun should be—
it's spring all right! It's spring!

N. M. Bodecker

44

Joyful

A summer day is full of ease,
a bank is full of money,
our lilac bush is full of bees,
and I am full of honey.

Rose Burgunder

Maytime Magic

A little seed
For me to sow . . .

A little earth
To make it grow . . .
A little hole,
A little pat . . .
A little wish,
And that is that.

A little sun,
A little shower . . .
A little while,
And then—a flower!

Mabel Watts

A Moment in Summer

A moment in summer
belongs to me
and one particular
honey bee.
A moment in summer
shimmering clear
making the sky
seem very near,
a moment in summer
belongs to me.

Charlotte Zolotow

Summer

When it's hot
I take my shoes off,
I take my shirt off,
I take my pants off,
I take my underwear off,
I take my whole body off,
and throw it
in the river.

Frank Asch

A Rocket in My Pocket

I've got a rocket
In my pocket;
I cannot stop to play.
Away it goes!
I've burned my toes.
It's Independence Day.

Anonymous

August

The sprinkler twirls.
   The summer wanes.
The pavement wears
   Popsicle stains.

The playground grass
   Is worn to dust.
The weary swings
   Creak, creak with rust.

The trees are bored
   With being green.
Some people leave
   The local scene

And go to seaside
   Bungalows
And take off nearly
   All their clothes.

John Updike

Harvest Home

The maples flare among the spruces,
The bursting foxgrape spills its juices,
The gentians lift their sapphire fringes
On roadways rich with golden tinges,
The waddling woodchucks fill their hampers,
The deer mouse runs, the chipmunk scampers,
The squirrels scurry, never stopping,
For all they hear is apples dropping
And walnuts plumping fast and faster;
The bee weighs down the purple aster—
Yes, hive your honey, little hummer,
The woods are waving, "Farewell, Summer."

Arthur Guiterman

October

In October
I'll be host
to witches, goblins
and a ghost.
I'll serve them
chicken soup
on toast.
Whoopy once
whoopy twice
whoopy chicken soup
with rice.

Maurice Sendak

October

October turned my maple's leaves to gold;
   The most are gone now; here and there one lingers.
Soon these will slip from out the twig's weak hold,
   Like coins between a dying miser's fingers.

Thomas Bailey Aldrich

This Is Halloween

Goblins on the doorstep,
   Phantoms in the air,
Owls on witches' gateposts
   Giving stare for stare,
Cats on flying broomsticks,
   Bats against the moon,
Stirrings round of fate-cakes
   With a solemn spoon,
Whirling apple parings,
   Figures draped in sheets
Dodging, disappearing,
   Up and down the streets,
Jack-o'-lanterns grinning,
   Shadows on a screen,
Shrieks and starts and laughter—
   This is Halloween!

Dorothy Brown Thompson

Lazy Witch

Lazy witch,
What's wrong with you?
   Get up and stir your magic brew.
   Here's candlelight to chase the gloom.
   Jump up and mount your flying broom
   And muster up your charms and spells
   And wicked grins and piercing yells.
   It's Halloween! There's work to do!
Lazy witch,
What's wrong with you?

Myra Cohn Livingston

Thanksgiving Magic

Thanksgiving Day I like to see
Our cook perform her witchery.
She turns a pumpkin into pie
As easily as you or I
Can wave a hand or wink an eye.
She takes leftover bread and muffin
And changes them to turkey stuffin'.
She changes cranberries to sauce
And meats to stews and stews to broths;
And when she mixes gingerbread
It turns into a man instead
With frosting collar 'round his throat
And raisin buttons down his coat.
Oh, some like magic made by wands,
   And some read magic out of books,
And some like fairy spells and charms
   But I like magic made by cooks!

Rowena Bastin Bennett

12 October

From where I stand now
   the world is flat,
   flat out flat,
   no end to that.

   Where my eyes go the land moves out.

How is it then
five hundred years ago (about)
Columbus found
that far beyond the flat on flat
the world was round?

Myra Cohn Livingston

Thanksgiving Day

Over the river and through the wood,
　To grandfather's house we go;
　　　The horse knows the way
　　　To carry the sleigh
　Through the white and drifted snow.

Over the river and through the wood—
　Oh, how the wind does blow!
　　　It stings the toes
　　　And bites the nose,
　As over the ground we go.

Over the river and through the wood,
　To have a first-rate play.
　　　Hear the bells ring,
　　　"Ting-a-ling-ding!"
　Hurrah for Thanksgiving Day!

Over the river and through the wood,
　Trot fast, my dapple-gray!
　　　Spring over the ground,
　　　Like a hunting-hound!
　For this is Thanksgiving Day.

Over the river and through the wood,
　And straight through the barn-yard gate.
　　　We seem to go
　　　Extremely slow—
　It is so hard to wait!

Over the river and through the wood—
　Now grandmother's cap I spy!
　　　Hurrah for the fun!
　　　Is the pudding done?
　Hurrah for the pumpkin-pie!

L. Maria Child

Thanksgiving

Thank You
　for all my hands can hold—
　　apples red,
　　　and melons gold,
　　　　yellow corn
　　　　　both ripe and sweet,
　　　　　peas and beans
　　　　　　so good to eat!

Thank You
　for all my eyes can see—
　　lovely sunlight,
　　　field and tree,
　　　　white cloud-boats
　　　　　in sea-deep sky,
　　　　　soaring bird
　　　　　　and butterfly.

Thank You
　for all my ears can hear—
　　birds' song echoing
　　　far and near,
　　　　songs of little
　　　　　stream, big sea,
　　　　　cricket, bullfrog,
　　　　　　duck and bee!

Ivy O. Eastwick

Light the Festive Candles
(FOR HANUKKAH)

Light the first of eight tonight—
the farthest candle to the right.

Light the first and second, too,
when tomorrow's day is through.

Then light three, and then light four—
every dusk one candle more

Till all eight burn bright and high,
honoring a day gone by

When the Temple was restored,
rescued from the Syrian lord,

And an eight-day feast proclaimed—
The Festival of Lights—well named

To celebrate the joyous day
when we regained the right to pray
to our one God in our own way.

Aileen Fisher

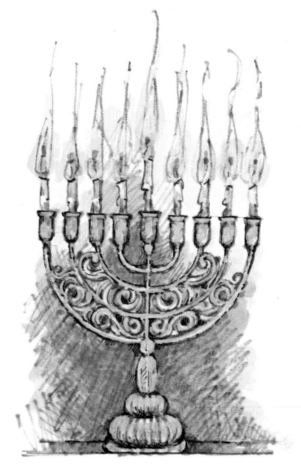

Winter Moon

How thin and sharp is the moon tonight!
How thin and sharp and ghostly white
Is the slim curved crook of the moon tonight!

Langston Hughes

The Children's Carol

Here we come again, again, and here we come again!
Christmas is a single pearl swinging on a chain,
Christmas is a single flower in a barren wood,
Christmas is a single sail on the salty flood,
Christmas is a single star in the empty sky,
Christmas is a single song sung for charity.
Here we come again, again, to sing to you again,
Give a single penny that we may not sing in vain.

Eleanor Farjeon

From: A Christmas Package
VIII

My stocking's where
He'll see it—there!
One-half a pair.

The tree is sprayed,
My prayers are prayed,
My wants are weighed.

I've made a list
Of what he missed
Last year. I've kissed

My father, mother,
Sister, brother;
I've done those other

Things I should
And would and could.
So far, so good.

David McCord

I Heard a Bird Sing

I heard a bird sing
    In the dark of December
A magical thing
    And sweet to remember.

"We are nearer to Spring
    Than we were in September,"
I heard a bird sing
    In the dark of December.

Oliver Herford

Merry Christmas

I saw on the snow
when I tried my skis
the track of a mouse
beside some trees.

Before he tunneled
to reach his house
he wrote "Merry Christmas"
in white, in mouse.

Aileen Fisher

A Visit from St. Nicholas

'Twas the night before Christmas, when all through the house
Not a creature was stirring, not even a mouse;
The stockings were hung by the chimney with care,
In hopes that St. Nicholas soon would be there;
The children were nestled all snug in their beds;
While visions of sugar-plums danced in their heads;
And mamma in her 'kerchief, and I in my cap,
Had just settled our brains for a long winter's nap—
When out on the lawn there arose such a clatter,
I sprang from my bed to see what was the matter.
Away to the window I flew like a flash,
Tore open the shutters, and threw up the sash.
The moon, on the breast of the new-fallen snow,
Gave the luster of midday to objects below;
When, what to my wondering eyes should appear,
but a miniature sleigh and eight tiny reindeer,
With a little old driver, so lively and quick,
I knew in a moment it must be St. Nick.
More rapid than eagles his coursers they came,
And he whistled, and shouted, and called them by name:
"Now, *Dasher*! now, *Dancer*! now, *Prancer* and *Vixen*!
On, *Comet*! on, *Cupid*! on, *Donder* and *Blitzen*!
To the top of the porch! to the top of the wall!
Now dash away! dash away! dash away all!"
As dry leaves that before the wild hurricane fly,
When they meet with an obstacle, mount to the sky;
So up to the house-top the coursers they flew
With the sleigh full of toys, and St. Nicholas too.

And then, in a twinkling, I heard on the roof
The prancing and pawing of each little hoof—
As I drew in my head, and was turning around,
Down the chimney St. Nicholas came with a bound.
He was dressed all in fur, from his head to his foot,
And his clothes were all tarnished with ashes and soot;
A bundle of toys he had flung on his back,
And he looked like a pedlar just opening his pack.
His eyes—how they twinkled; his dimples, how merry!
His cheeks were like roses, his nose like a cherry!
His droll little mouth was drawn up like a bow,
And the beard of his chin was as white as the snow;
The stump of a pipe he held tight in his teeth,
And the smoke it encircled his head like a wreath;
He had a broad face and a little round belly
That shook, when he laughed, like a bowl full of jelly.
He was chubby and plump, a right jolly old elf,
And I laughed when I saw him, in spite of myself;
A wink of his eye and a twist of his head
Soon gave me to know I had nothing to dread;
He spoke not a word, but went straight to his work,
And filled all the stockings; then turned with a jerk,
And laying his finger aside of his nose,
And giving a nod, up the chimney he rose;
He sprang to his sleigh, to his team gave a whistle,
And away they all flew like the down of a thistle.
But I heard him exclaim, ere he drove out of sight,
Happy Christmas to all, and to all a good night!"

Clement Clarke Moore

DOGS AND CATS AND BEARS AND BATS

Mammals are a varied lot;
some are furry, some are not;
many come equipped with tails;
some have quills, a few have scales.

Some are large, and others small;
some are quick, while others crawl;
they prance on land, they swing from trees;
they're underground and in the seas.

Some have hooves, and some have paws;
some have fangs in snapping jaws;
some will snarl if you come near;
others quickly disappear.

Dogs and cats and bears and bats,
all are mammals, so are rats;
whales are mammals, camels too;
I'm a mammal . . . so are YOU!

Mice

I think mice
Are rather nice.

Their tails are long,
Their faces small,
They haven't any
Chins at all.
Their ears are pink,
Their teeth are white,
They run about
The house at night.
They nibble things
They shouldn't touch
And no one seems
To like them much.

But *I* think mice
Are nice.

Rose Fyleman

The Waltzer in the House

A sweet, a delicate white mouse,
A little blossom of a beast,
Is waltzing in the house
Among the crackers and the yeast.

O the swaying of his legs!
O the bobbing of his head!
The lady, beautiful and kind,
The blue-eyed mistress, lately wed,
Has almost laughed away her wits
To see the pretty mouse that sits
On his tiny pink behind
And swaying, bobbing, begs.

She feeds him tarts and curds,
Seed packaged for the birds,
And figs, and nuts, and cheese;
Polite as Pompadour to please
The dainty waltzer of her house,
The sweet, the delicate, the innocent white mouse.

As in a dream, as in a trance,
She loves his rhythmic elegance,
She laughs to see his bobbing dance.

Stanley Kunitz

The Rabbit

When they said the time to hide was mine,
I hid back under a thick grape vine.

And while I was still for the time to pass,
A little gray thing came out of the grass.

He hopped his way through the melon bed
And sat down close by a cabbage head.

He sat down close where I could see,
And his big still eyes looked hard at me,

His big eyes bursting out of the rim,
And I looked back very hard at him.

Elizabeth Madox Roberts

To a Squirrel at Kyle-Na-No

Come play with me;
Why should you run
Through the shaking tree
As though I'd a gun
To strike you dead?
When all I would do
Is to scratch your head
And let you go.

William Butler Yeats

The Chipmunk's Day

In and out the bushes, up the ivy,
Into the hole
By the old oak stump, the chipmunk flashes
Up the pole.

To the feeder full of seeds he dashes,
Stuffs his cheeks,
The chickadee and titmouse scold him.
Down he streaks.

Red as the leaves the wind blows off the maple,
Red as a fox,
Striped like a skunk, the chipmunk whistles
Past the love seat, past the mailbox,

Down the path,
Home to his warm hole stuffed with sweet
Things to eat.
Neat and slight and shining, his front feet

Curled at his breast, he sits there while the sun
Stripes the red west
With its last light: the chipmunk
Dives to his rest.

Randall Jarrell

The Hedgehog

The Hedgehog sleeps beneath the hedge—
    As you may sometimes see—
And I prefer it sleeping there
    To sleeping here with me!

J. J. Bell

The Bat

Bats are creepy; bats are scary;
Bats do not seem sanitary;
Bats in dismal caves keep cozy;
Bats remind us of Lugosi;
Bats have webby wings that fold up;
Bats from ceilings hang down rolled up
Bats when flying undismayed are;
Bats are careful; bats use radar;
Bats at nighttime at their best are;
Bats by Batman unimpressed are!

Frank Jacobs

The Bat

By day the bat is cousin to the mouse.
He likes the attic of an ageing house.

His fingers make a hat about his head.
His pulse beat is so slow we think him dead.

He loops in crazy figures half the night
Among the trees that face the corner light.

But when he brushes up against a screen,
We are afraid of what our eyes have seen:

For something is amiss or out of place
When mice with wings can wear a human face.

Theodore Roethke

The Sloth

In moving-slow he has no Peer.
You ask him something in his ear;
He thinks about it for a Year;

And, then, before he says a Word
There, upside down (unlike a Bird)
He will assume that you have Heard-

A most Ex-as-per-at-ing Lug.
But should you call his manner Smug
He'll sigh and give his Branch a Hug;

Then off again to Sleep he goes,
Still swaying gently by his Toes,
And you just *know* he knows he kno

Theodore Roeth

Camel

am a camel in all the sand.
do not require a helping hand.

Near where my camel-master sits
s a great big statue shattered into bits.

My hump is solid, my hoofs are tough;
My personality is gruff.

'm endlessly stubborn and stupidly slow.
invariably know the way to go.

Alan Brownjohn

The Camel's Complaint

"Canary-birds feed on sugar and seed,
    Parrots have crackers to crunch;
And, as for the poodles, they tell me the noodles
    Have chickens and cream for their lunch.
        But there's never a question
        About MY digestion—
    ANYTHING does for me!

"Cats, you're aware, can repose in a chair,
    Chickens can roost upon rails;
Puppies are able to sleep in a stable,
    And oysters can slumber in pails.
        But no one supposes
        A poor Camel dozes—
    ANY PLACE does for me!

"Lambs are inclosed where it's never exposed,
    Coops are constructed for hens;
Kittens are treated to houses well heated,
    And pigs are protected by pens.
        But a Camel comes handy
        Wherever it's sandy—
    ANYWHERE does for me!

"People would laugh if you rode a giraffe,
    Or mounted the back of an ox;
It's nobody's habit to ride on a rabbit,
    Or try to bestraddle a fox.
        But as for a Camel, he's
        Ridden by families—
    ANY LOAD does for me!

"A snake is as round as a hole in the ground,
    And weasels are wavy and sleek;
And no alligator could ever be straighter
    Than lizards that live in a creek.
        But a Camel's all lumpy
        And bumpy and humpy—
    ANY SHAPE does for me!"

Charles Edward Carryl

Buffalo Dusk

The buffaloes are gone.
And those who saw the buffaloes are gone.
Those who saw the buffaloes by thousands and how they
    pawed the prairie sod into dust with their great hoofs
    their great heads down pawing on in a great pageant
    of dusk,
Those who saw the buffaloes are gone.
And the buffaloes are gone.

Carl Sandburg

The Hippopotamus

The huge hippopotamus hasn't a hair
on the back of his wrinkly hide;
he carries the bulk of his prominent hulk
rather loosely assembled inside.

The huge hippopotamus lives without care
at a slow philosophical pace,
as he wades in the mud with a thump and a thud
and a permanent grin on his face.

Jack Prelutsky

Holding Hands

Elephants walking
Along the trails

Are holding hands
By holding tails

Trunks and tails
Are handy things

When elephants walk
In circus rings.

Elephants work
And elephants play

And elephants walk
And feel so gay.

And when they walk—
It never fails

They're holding hands
By holding tails.

Lenore M. Link

Beside the Line of Elephants

I think they had no pattern
   When they cut out the elephant's skin;
Some places it needs letting out,
   And others, taking in.

Edna Becker

Oliphaunt

Gray as a mouse,
Big as a house,
Nose like a snake,
I make the earth shake,
As I tramp through the grass;
Trees crack as I pass.
With horns in my mouth
I walk in the South,
Flapping big ears.
Beyond count of years
I stump round and round,
Never lie on the ground,
Not even to die.
Oliphaunt am I,
Biggest of all,
Huge, old, and tall.
If ever you'd met me,
You wouldn't forget me.
If you never do,
You won't think I'm true;
But old Oliphaunt am I,
And I never lie.

J. R. R. Tolkien

The Wolf

When the pale moon hides and the wild wind wails,
And over the tree-tops the nighthawk sails,
The gray wolf sits on the world's far rim,
And howls: and it seems to comfort him.

The wolf is a lonely soul, you see,
No beast in the wood, nor bird in the tree,
But shuns his path; in the windy gloom
They give him plenty, and plenty of room.

So he sits with his long, lean face to the sky
Watching the ragged clouds go by.
There in the night, alone, apart,
Singing the song of his lone, wild heart.

Far away, on the world's dark rim
He howls, and it seems to comfort him.

Georgia Roberts Durston

Four Little Foxes

Speak gently, Spring, and make no sudden sound;
For in my windy valley, yesterday, I found
New-born foxes squirming on the ground—
                 Speak gently.

Walk softly, March, forbear the bitter blow;
Her feet within a trap, her blood upon the snow,
The four little foxes saw their mother go—
                 Walk softly.

Go lightly, Spring, oh, give them no alarm;
When I covered them with boughs to shelter them from harm,
The thin blue foxes suckled at my arm—
                 Go lightly.

Step softly, March, with your rampant hurricane;
Nuzzling one another, and whimpering with pain,
The new little foxes are shivering in the rain—
                 Step softly.

Lew Sarett

Grandpa Bear's Lullaby

The night is long
But fur is deep.
You will be warm
In winter sleep.

The food is gone
But dreams are sweet
And they will be
Your winter meat.

The cave is dark
But dreams are bright
And they will serve
As winter light.

Sleep, my little cubs, sleep.

Jane Yolen

The Lesser Lynx

The laughter of the Lesser Lynx
   Is often insincere:
It pays to be polite, he thinks,
   If Royalty is near.

So when the Lion steals his food
   Or kicks him from behind,
He smiles, of course—but oh, the rude
   Remarks that cross his mind!

E. V. Rieu

Polar Bear

The secret of the polar bear
Is that he wears long underwear.

Gail Kredenser

Leopard

Eons ago, when the earth was still yeasty,
The leopard, my love, was an unspotted beasty,
Unsullied as sunlight, not one spot or two spots.
Alas! He was snared for the simmering stew pots!
But too many cooks shaking shakers of spices
Created a much needed moment of crisis.
He leaped for his life while the cooks were kerchooing
And fled, all the fleet-footed natives pursuing.
He escaped! But his fur was still salted and peppered,
And that's how there came to be spots on the leopard.

Gretchen Kreps

Lion

The lion, ruler over all the beasts,
Triumphant moves upon the grassy plain
With sun like gold upon his tawny brow
And dew like silver on his shaggy mane.

Into himself he draws the rolling thunder,
Beneath his flinty paw great boulders quake;
He will dispatch the mouse to burrow under,
The little deer to shiver in the brake.

He sets the fierce whip of each serpent lashing,
The tall giraffe brings humbly to his knees,
Awakes the sloth, and sends the wild boar crashing,
Wide-eyed monkeys chittering, through the trees.

He gazes down into the quiet river,
Parting the green bulrushes to behold
A sunflower-crown of amethyst and silver,
A royal coat of brushed and beaten gold.

William Jay Smith

The Lion

The lion has a golden mane
and under it a clever brain.
He lies around and idly roars
and lets the lioness do the chores.

Jack Prelutsky

Seal

See how he dives
From the rocks with a zoom!
See how he darts
Through his watery room
Past crabs and eels
And green seaweed,
Past fluffs of sandy
Minnow feed!
See how he swims
With a swerve and a twist,
A flip of the flipper,
A flick of the wrist!
Quicksilver-quick,
Softer than spray,
Down he plunges
And sweeps away;
Before you can think,
Before you can utter
Words like "Dill pickle"
Or "Apple butter,"
Back up he swims
Past Sting Ray and Shark,
Out with a zoom,
A whoop, a bark;
Before you can say
Whatever you wish,
He plops at your side
With a mouthful of fish!

William Jay Smith

The Mandrill

In the Mandrill
unrefined
Beauty and Beast
are well combined.
How would *you* like
to have that face
to look at in your looking-glass?
And all the other
jungle creatures
what must *they* think
of those strange features?
And that odd name
the Mandrill—can
it be he hopes
to BE a *man*?
But *that* face
won't
wash
off
with
soap:
I fear poor Mandrill
has
no
hope.

       Conrad Aiken

The Performing Seal

Who is so proud
As not to feel
A secret awe
Before a seal
That keeps such sleek
And wet repose
While twirling candles
On his nose?

      Rachel Field

The Wild, the Free

With flowing tail, and flying mane,
Wide nostrils never stretched by pain,
Mouths bloodless to the bit or rein,
And feet that iron never shod,
And flanks unscarred by spur or rod,
A thousand horse, the wild, the free,
Like waves that follow o'er the sea.

      Lord Byron

The Donkey

I saw a donkey
  One day old,
His head was too big
  For his neck to hold;
His legs were shaky
  And long and loose,
They rocked and staggered
  And weren't much use.
He tried to gambol
  And frisk a bit,
But he wasn't quite sure
  Of the trick of it.
His queer little coat
  Was soft and gray
And curled at his neck
  In a lovely way.
His face was wistful
  And left no doubt
That he felt life needed
  Some thinking about.
So he blundered round
  In venturesome quest,
And then lay flat
  On the ground to rest.
He looked so little
  And weak and slim,
I prayed the world
  Might be good to him.

      Anonymous

Ode to the Pig: His Tail

My tail is not impressive
    But it's elegant and neat.
In length it's not excessive—
    I can't curl it round my feet—
But it's awfully expressive
And its weight is not excessive,
    And I *don't* think it's conceit,
    Or foolishly possessive
If I state with some aggressive-
    ness that it's the final master touch
That makes a pig complete.

Walter R. Brooks

The Pig

The pig is not a nervous beast;
He never worries in the least.
He lives his tranquil life unshaken,
And when he dies brings home the bacon.

Roland Young

The Hairy Dog

My dog's so furry I've not seen
His face for years and years:
His eyes are buried out of sight,
I only guess his ears.

When people ask me for his breed,
I do not know or care:
He has the beauty of them all
Hidden beneath his hair.

Herbert Asquith

A Pig Is Never Blamed

A pig is never blamed in case
he forgets to wash his face.
No dirty suds are on his soap,
because with soap he does not cope.
He never has to clean the tub
after he has had a scrub,
for whatever mess he makes,
a bath is what he never takes.
But then, what is a pool to him?
Poor pig, he never learns to swim.
And all the goodies he can cram
down his gullet turn to ham.
It's mean:
keeping clean.
You hardly want to, till you're very big.
But it's worse to be a pig.

Babette Deutsch

The Cow

The cow is of the bovine ilk;
One end is moo, the other, milk.

Ogden Nash

Roger the Dog

Asleep he wheezes at his ease.
He only wakes to scratch his fleas.

He hogs the fire, he bakes his head
As if it were a loaf of bread.

He's just a sack of snoring dog.
You can lug him like a log.

You can roll him with your foot,
He'll stay snoring where he's put.

I take him out for exercise,
He rolls in cowclap up to his eyes.

He will not race, he will not romp,
He saves his strength for gobble and chomp.

He'll work as hard as you could wish
Emptying his dinner dish,

Then flops flat, and digs down deep,
Like a miner, into sleep.

Ted Hughes

Lone Dog

I'm a lean dog, a keen dog, a wild dog and lone,
I'm a rough dog, a tough dog, hunting on my own!
I'm a bad dog, a mad dog, teasing silly sheep;
I love to sit and bay at the moon and keep fat souls from sleep.

I'll never be a lap dog, licking dirty feet,
A sleek dog, a meek dog, cringing for my meat.
Not for me the fireside, the well-filled plate,
But shut door and sharp stone and cuff and kick and hate.

Not for me the other dogs, running by my side,
Some have run a short while, but none of them would bide.
O mine is still the lone trail, the hard trail, the best,
Wide wind and wild stars and the hunger of the quest.

Irene McLeod

I've Got a Dog

I've got a dog as thin as a rail,
He's got fleas all over his tail;
Every time his tail goes flop,
The fleas on the bottom all hop to the top.

Anonymous

Bliss

Let me fetch sticks,
Let me fetch stones,
Throw me your bones,
Teach me your tricks.

When you go ride,
Let me go run,
You in the sun,
Me at your side;

When you go swim,
Let me go too
Both lost in blue
Up to the brim;

Let me do this,
Let me do that—
What you are at,
That is my bliss.

Eleanor Farjeon

His Highness's Dog

I am his Highness's dog at Kew;
Pray, tell me, sir, whose dog are you?

Anonymous

Sunning

Old Dog lay in the summer sun
Much too lazy to rise and run.
He flapped an ear
At a buzzing fly.
He winked a half opened
Sleepy eye.
He scratched himself
On an itching spot,
As he dozed on the porch
Where the sun was hot.
He whimpered a bit
From force of habit
While he lazily dreamed
Of chasing a rabbit.
But Old Dog happily lay in the sun
Much too lazy to rise and run.

James S. Tippett

The Cat of Cats

I am the cat of cats. I am
   The everlasting cat!
Cunning, and old, and sleek as jam,
   The everlasting cat!
I hunt the vermin in the night—
   The everlasting cat!
For I see best without the light—
   The everlasting cat!

William Brighty Rands

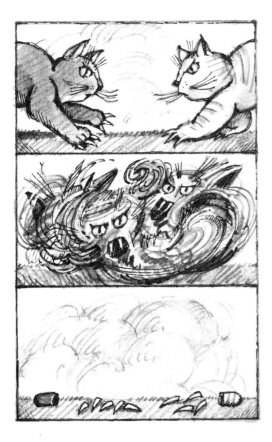

The Cats of Kilkenny

There were once two cats of Kilkenny,
Each thought there was one cat too many;
So they fought and they fit,
And they scratched and they bit,
Till, excepting their nails
And the tips of their tails,
Instead of two cats, there weren't any.

Anonymous

A Cat in Despondency

A cat in despondency sighed
And resolved to commit suicide.
   She passed under the wheels
   Of eight automobiles,
And under the ninth one she died.

Anonymous

Country Barnyard

Cats and kittens, kittens and cats
under the barn and under the shed;
a face by the steps, a tail by the ramp
and off they go, if they hear a tread!

Sleep in the sun with one eye on guard,
doze in the grass with a listening ear,
run for the darkness under the barn
as soon as a human being draws near!

Not quite wild and not quite tame,
thin and limber, with hungry eye:
the house cat sits at the kitchen door
disdainfully watching her kin go by.

Elizabeth Coatsworth

Cats

Cats sleep
Anywhere,
Any table,
Any chair,
Top of piano,
Window-ledge,
In the middle,
On the edge,
Open drawer,
Empty shoe,
Anybody's
Lap will do,
Fitted in a
Cardboard box,
In the cupboard
With your frocks—
Anywhere!
They don't care!
Cats sleep
Anywhere.

Eleanor Farjeon

Cat

The black cat yawns,
Opens her jaws,
Stretches her legs,
And shows her claws.

Then she gets up
And stands on four
Long stiff legs
And yawns some more.

She shows her sharp teeth,
She stretches her lip,
Her slice of a tongue
Turns up at the tip.

Lifting herself
On her delicate toes,
She arches her back
As high as it goes.

She lets herself down
With particular care,
And pads away
With her tail in the air.

Mary Britton Miller

Little Things

Little things, that run, and quail,
And die, in silence and despair!

Little things, that fight, and fail,
And fall, on sea, and earth, and air!

All trapped and frightened little things,
The mouse, the coney, hear our prayer!

As we forgive those done to us,
—The lamb, the linnet, and the hare—

Forgive us all our trespasses,
Little creatures, everywhere!

James Stephens

Cat's Menu

I eat what I wish—
It's a matter of taste.
Whether liver or fish,
I eat what I wish.
Putting scraps in my dish
Is a terrible waste.
I eat what I wish—
It's a matter of taste.

Richard Shaw

Feather or Fur

When you watch for
Feather or fur
Feather or fur
Do not stir
Do not stir.

Feather or fur
Come crawling
Creeping
Some come peeping
Some by night
And some by day.
Most come gently
All come softly
Do not scare
A friend away.

When you watch for
Feather or fur
Feather or fur
Do not stir
Do not stir.

John Becker

THE WAYS OF LIVING THINGS

There is wonder past all wonder
in the ways of living things,
in a worm's intrepid wriggling,
in the song a blackbird sings,

In the grandeur of an eagle
and the fury of a shark,
in the calmness of a tortoise
on a meadow in the dark,

In the splendor of a sea gull
as it plummets from the sky,
in the incandescent shimmer
of a noisy dragonfly,

In a heron, still and silent
underneath a crescent moon,
in a butterfly emerging
from its silver-spun cocoon.

In a fish's joyful splashing,
in a snake that makes no sound,
in the smallest salamander
there is wonder to be found.

Hurt No Living Thing

Hurt no living thing;
Ladybird, nor butterfly,
Nor moth with dusty wing,
Nor cricket chirping cheerily,
Nor grasshopper so light of leap,
Nor dancing gnat, nor beetle fat,
Nor harmless worms that creep.

Christina Rossetti

Green Stems

Little things that crawl and creep
In the green grass forests,
Deep in their long-stemmed world
Where ferns uncurl
To a greener world
Beneath the leaves above them;
And every flower upon its stem
Blows above them there
The bottom of a geranium,
The back side of a trillium,
The belly of a bumblebee
Is all they see, these little things
Down so low
Where no bird sings
Where no winds blow,
Deep in their long-stemmed world.

Margaret Wise Brown

Hey, Bug!

Hey, bug, stay!
Don't run away.
I know a game that we can play.

I'll hold my fingers very still
and you can climb a finger-hill.

No, no.
Don't go.

Here's a wall—a tower, too,
a tiny bug town, just for you.
I've a cookie. You have some.
Take this oatmeal cookie crumb.

Hey, bug, stay!
Hey, bug!
Hey!

Lilian Moore

Praying Mantis

That praying mantis over there
Is really not engaged in prayer.
That praying mantis that you see
Is really preying (with an "e").
It preys upon the garter snake.
It preys upon the bumblebee.
It preys upon the cabbage worm,
The wasp, the fly, the moth, the flea.
(And sometimes, if its need is great,
It even preys upon its mate.)

With prey and preying both so endless,
It tends to end up rather friendless
And seldom is commended much
Except by gardeners and such.

Mary Ann Hoberman

Crickets

Crickets
Talk
In the tall
Grass
All
Late summer
Long.
When
Summer
Is gone,
The dry
Grass
Whispers
Alone.

Valerie Worth

A Bug Sat in a Silver Flower

A bug sat in a silver flower
Thinking silver thoughts.
A bigger bug out for a walk
Climbed up that silver flower stalk
And snapped the small bug down his jaws
Without a pause
Without a care
For all the bug's small silver thoughts.
It isn't right
It isn't fair
That big bug ate that little bug
Because that little bug was there.

He also ate his underwear.

Karla Kuskin

Ants, Although Admirable, Are Awfully Aggravating

The busy ant works hard all day
And never stops to rest or play.
He carries things ten times his size,
And never grumbles, whines or cries.
And even climbing flower stalks,
He always runs, he never walks.
He loves his work, he never tires,
And never puffs, pants or perspires.

Yet though I praise his boundless vim
I am not really fond of him.

Walter R. Brooks

Bug in a Jug

Curious fly,
Vinegar jug,
Slippery edge,
Pickled bug.

Anonymous

The Bug

And when the rain had gone away
And it was shining everywhere,
I ran out on the walk to play
And found a little bug was there.

And he was running just as fast
As any little bug could run,
Until he stopped for breath at last,
All black and shiny in the sun.

And then he chirped a song to me
And gave his wings a little tug,
And *that's* the way he showed that he
Was very glad to be a bug!

Marjorie Barrows

Wasps

Wasps like coffee.
Syrup.
Tea.
Coca-Cola.
Butter.
Me.

Dorothy Aldis

The Flea

And here's the happy, bounding flea—
You cannot tell the he from she.
The sexes look alike, you see;
But she can tell and so can he.

Roland Young

Oh the Toe-Test!

The fly, the fly,
in the wink of an eye,
can taste with his feet
if the syrup is sweet
or the bacon is salty.
Oh is it his fault he
gets toast on his toes
as he tastes as he goes?

Norma Farber

Cockroaches

A leaf bug comes from an egg in June
Before it can live and thrive.
A green moth comes from a curled cocoon,
A honeybee from a hive.
But though in all of the insect books
Such varied sources make sense,
Like water beetles coming from brooks
Or caterpillars from tents . . .
The thing that really puzzles me some
In the way of bug affairs
Is: why do cockroaches always come
From The People Living Upstairs?

Kaye Starbird

When Mosquitoes Make a Meal

When mosquitoes make a meal,
Arms and legs have great appeal.

But they stay out when we go in.
That's why mosquitoes are so thin.

And if we keep them from their dinner,
They're bound to grow a great deal thinner.

Else Holmelund Minarik

A Dragonfly

When the heat of the summer
Made drowsy the land,
A dragonfly came
And sat on my hand.

With its blue-jointed body,
And wings like spun glass,
It lit on my fingers
As though they were grass.

Eleanor Farjeon

The Tickle Rhyme

"Who's that tickling my back?" said the wall
    "Me," said a small
Caterpillar. "I'm learning
To crawl."

Ian Serraillier

Fireflies in the Garden

Here come real stars to fill the upper skies,
And here on earth come emulating flies,
That though they never equal stars in size,
(And they were never really stars at heart)
Achieve at times a very star-like start.
Only, of course, they can't sustain the part.

Robert Frost

Caterpillar

Brown and furry
Caterpillar in a hurry,
Take your walk
To the shady leaf, or stalk,
Or what not,
Which may be the chosen spot.
No toad spy you,
Hovering bird of prey pass by you;
Spin and die,
To live again a butterfly.

Christina Rossetti

Ladybug

A small speckled visitor
        wearing crimson cape,
brighter than a cherry,
        smaller than a grape.

A polka-dotted someone
        walking on my wall,
a black-hooded lady
        in a scarlet shawl.

Joan Walsh Anglund

The Flattered Flying Fish

Said the Shark to the Flying Fish over the phone:
"Will you join me tonight? I am dining alone.
Let me order a nice little dinner for two!
And come as you are, in your shimmering blue."

Said the Flying Fish: "Fancy remembering me,
And the dress that I wore at the Porpoises' tea!"
"How could I forget?" said the Shark in his guile:
"I expect you at eight!" and rang off with a smile.

She has powdered her nose; she has put on her things;
She is off with one flap of her luminous wings.
O little one, lovely, light-hearted and vain,
The Moon will not shine on your beauty again!

E.V. Rieu

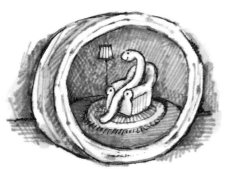

A Wee Little Worm

A wee little worm in a hickory-nut
    Sang, happy as he could be,
"O I live in the heart of the whole round world,
    And it all belongs to me!"

James Whitcomb Riley

The Codfish

The codfish lays ten thousand eggs,
    The homely hen lays one.
The codfish never cackles
    To tell you what she's done.
And so we scorn the codfish,
    While the humble hen we prize,
Which only goes to show you
    That it pays to advertise.

Anonymous

Long Gone

Don't waste your time in looking for
the long-extinct tyrannosaur,
because this ancient dinosaur
just can't be found here anymore.

This also goes for stegosaurus,
allosaurus, brontosaurus
and any other saur or saurus.
They all lived here long before us.

Jack Prelutsky

The Shark

A treacherous monster is the Shark,
He never makes the least remark.

And when he sees you on the sand,
He doesn't seem to want to land.

He watches you take off your clothes,
And not the least excitement shows.

His eyes do not grow bright or roll,
He has astounding self-control.

He waits till you are quite undressed,
And seems to take no interest.

And when towards the sea you leap,
He looks as if he were asleep.

But when you once get in his range,
His whole demeanor seems to change.

He throws his body right about,
And his true character comes out.

It's no use crying or appealing,
He seems to lose all decent feeling.

After this warning you will wish
To keep clear of this treacherous fish.

His back is black, his stomach white,
He has a very dangerous bite.

Lord Alfred Douglas

Fishes' Evening Song

Flip flop,
Flip flap,
Slip slap,
Lip lap;
Water sounds,
Soothing sounds.
We fan our fins
As we lie
Resting here
Eye to eye.
Water falls
Drop by drop,
Plip plop,
Drip drop.
Plink plunk,
Splash splish;
Fish fins fan,
Fish tails swish,
Swush, swash, swish.
This we wish . . .
Water cold,
Water clear,
Water smooth,
Just to soothe
Sleepy fish.

Dahlov Ipcar

Brontosaurus

The giant brontosaurus
Was a prehistoric chap
With four fat feet to stand on
And a very skimpy lap.
The scientists assure us
Of a most amazing thing—
A brontosaurus blossomed
When he had a chance to sing!

(The bigger brontosauruses,
Who liked to sing in choruses,
Would close their eyes
and harmonize
And sing most anything.)

They growled and they yowled,
They deedled and they dummed;
They warbled and they whistled,
They howled and they hummed.
They didn't eat, they didn't sleep;
They sang and sang all day.
Now all you'll find are footprints
Where they tapped the time away!

Gail Kredenser

ly and Manda

y and Manda are two little lizards
Who gobble up flies in their two little gizzards.
y live by a toadstool near two little hummocks
nd crawl all around on their two little stomachs.

Alice B. Campbell

The Boa

Allow me just one short remark
   About this lengthy Boa:
If Noah had it in his ark,
   I sympathize with Noah!

J. J. Bell

The Lizard

The Lizard is a timid thing
That cannot dance or fly or sing;
He hunts for bugs beneath the floor
And longs to be a dinosaur.

John Gardner

Desert Tortoise

I am the *old* one here.

Mice
and snakes
and deer
and butterflies
and badgers
come and go.
Centipedes
and eagles
come and go.

But tortoises
grow old
and *stay.*

Our lives stretch out.

I cross
the same arroyo
that I crossed
when I was young,
returning to
the same safe den
to sleep through
winter's cold.
Each spring,
I warm myself
in the same sun,
search for the same
long tender blades
of green,
and taste the same
ripe juicy cactus fruit.

I know
the slow
sure way
my world
repeats itself.
I know
how I fit in.

My shell still shows
the toothmarks
where a wildcat
thought he had me
long ago.
He didn't know
that I was safe
beneath
the hard brown rock
he tried to bite.

I trust that shell.
I move
at my own speed.

This
is a good place
for an old tortoise
to walk.

Byrd Baylor

Samuel

I found this salamander
Near the pond in the wood.
Samuel, I called him—
Samuel, Samuel.
Right away I loved him.
He loved me too, I think.
Samuel, I called him—
Samuel, Samuel.

I took him home in a coffee can,
And at night
He slept in my bed.
In the morning
I took him to school.

He died very quietly during spelling.

Sometimes I think
I should have left him
Near the pond in the woods.
Samuel, I called him—
Samuel, Samuel.

Bobbi Katz

The Crocodile

How doth the little crocodile
    Improve his shining tail,
And pour the waters of the Nile
    On every golden scale!

How cheerfully he seems to grin!
    How neatly spread his claws,
And welcomes little fishes in
    With gently smiling jaws!

Lewis Carroll

The Frog

Be kind and tender to the Frog,
    And do not call him names,
As "Slimy skin," or "Polly-wog,"
    Or likewise "Ugly James,"
Or "Gape-a-grin," or "Toad-gone-wrong,"
    Or "Billy Bandy-knees":
The Frog is justly sensitive
    To epithets like these.
No animal will more repay
    A treatment kind and fair;
At least so lonely people say
Who keep a frog (and, by the way,
    They are extremely rare).

Hilaire Belloc

The Tree Frog

The tree frog
Creaks and croaks and croaks
And says "Dee deep"
On elms and oaks,
"Dee deep," he says
And stops, till when
It's time to say
"Dee deep" again.

John Travers Moore

The Polliwog

Oh, the Polliwog is woggling
   In his pleasant native bog
With his beady eyes a-gogglin
   Through the underwater fo
And his busy tail a-joggling
   And his eager head agog—
Just a happy little frogling
   Who is bound to be a Frog

Arthur Guiterman

The Hummingbird

The Hummingbird, he has no song
From flower to flower he hums along
Humming his way among the trees
He finds no words for what he sees

Michael Flanders

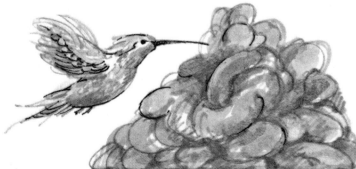

Baby Talk

The fledglings have a language
   That is all their own.
They lisp in broken syllables
   In a high, clear tone.
Each bird learns first a single wor
   Quite long for a beginner,
But says it very plainly,
   "Dinner
     Dinner
       Dinner."

Anna Bird Stewart

The Canary

The song of canaries
Never varies,
And when they're moulting
They're pretty revolting.

Ogden Nash

The Blackbird

In the far corner
close by the swings,
every morning
a blackbird sings.

His bill's so yellow,
his coat's so black,
that he makes a fellow
whistle back.

Ann, my daughter,
thinks that he
sings for us two
especially.

Humbert Wolfe

Ducks' Ditty

All along the backwater,
Through the rushes tall,
Ducks are a-dabbling.
Up tails all!

Ducks' tails, drakes' tails,
Yellow feet a-quiver,
Yellow bills all out of sight
Busy in the river!

Slushy green undergrowth
Where the roach swim—
Here we keep our larder,
Cool and full and dim.

Every one for what he likes!
We like to be
Head down, tails up,
Dabbling free!

High in the blue above
Swifts whirl and call—
We are down a-dabbling
Up tails all!

Kenneth Grahame

The Duck

When you're a Duck like me it's impossible
to make friends with humans like you.
We're friendly and don't cause any trouble,
but you're not and you certainly do.

We swim round, me and the family,
while you throw us old lumps of bread.
Your dog starts to run with the crack of your gun
and one of us loses his head.

And if that's not enough, then you cook us
with our legs sticking up in the air.
Try putting yourself into our place.
I tell you, it just isn't fair.

Richard Digance

Sea Gull

The sea gull curves his wings,
the sea gull turns his eyes.
Get down into the water, fish!
(if you are wise.)

The sea gull slants his wings,
the sea gull turns his head.
Get deep into the water, fish!
(or you'll be dead.)

Elizabeth Coatsworth

The Sandpiper

At the edge of tide
He stops to wonder,
Races through
The lace of thunder.

On toothpick legs
Swift and brittle,
He runs and pipes
And his voice is little.

But small or not,
He has a notion
To outshout
The Atlantic Ocean.

Frances Frost

The Sandpiper

Along the sea-edge, like a gnome
Or rolling pebble in the foam,
As though he timed the ocean's throbbing
Runs a piper, bobbing, bobbing.

Now he stiffens, now he wilts,
Like a little boy on stilts!
Creatures burrow, insects hide,
When they see the piper glide.

You would think him out of joint,
Till his bill began to point.
You would doubt if he could fly,
Till his straightness arrows by.

You would take him for a clown,`
Till he peeps and flutters down,
Vigilant among the grasses,
Where a fledgling bobs and passes.

Witter Bynner

The Hen

The Hen is a ferocious fowl,
She pecks you till she makes you howl.

And all the time she flaps her wings,
And says the most insulting things.

And when you try to take her eggs,
She bites large pieces from your legs.

The only safe way to get these,
Is to creep on your hands and knees.

In the meanwhile a friend must hide,
And jump out on the other side.

And then you snatch the eggs and run,
While she pursues the other one.

The difficulty is, to find
A trusty friend who will not mind.

Lord Alfred Douglas

Something Told the Wild Geese

Something told the wild geese
    It was time to go.
Though the fields lay golden
    Something whispered—"Snow."
Leaves were green and stirring,
    Berries, luster-glossed,
But beneath warm feathers
    Something cautioned—"Frost."
All the sagging orchards
    Steamed with amber spice,
But each wild breast stiffened
    At remembered ice.
Something told the wild geese
    It was time to fly—
Summer sun was on their wings,
    Winter in their cry.

Rachel Field

Night Heron

Hunting my cat along the evening brook
Where she'd been stalking deer mice in the weeds,
I nearly missed this sight—the great night heron
Bluer than dusk in the maze of willow reeds.

Beautiful, motionless, he stood in silence
On one leg, waiting for lantern flies,
And gazed across the brook to where in hemlock
His nest of sticks rose high against the skies.

Then at my feet I saw my fierce young hunter
Crouched in the wet grass, trembling and in awe.
We left our heron to his stars. Cat shivered
And touched my cheek with a damp and golden paw.

Frances Frost

The Vulture

The Vulture eats between his meals
  And that's the reason why
He very, very rarely feels
  As well as you and I.

His eye is dull, his head is bald,
  His neck is growing thinner.
Oh! what a lesson for us all
  To only eat at dinner!

Hilaire Belloc

The Eagle

He clasps the crag with crooked hands;
Close to the sun in lonely lands,
Ringed with the azure world, he stands.

The wrinkled sea beneath him crawls;
He watches from his mountain walls,
And like a thunderbolt he falls.

Alfred Tennyson

The Sparrow Hawk

Wings like pistols flashing at his sides,
Masked, above the meadow runway rides,
Galloping, galloping with an easy rein.
Below, the fieldmouse, where the shadow glides,
Holds fast the small purse of his life, and hides.

Russell Hoban

CITY, OH, CITY!

City, oh, city
of glory and grace,
of breathtaking towers
that soar into space,
of bottomless canyons,
steel, rivet, and stone;
City, oh, city,
how mighty you've grown.

City, oh, city
of myriad ways,
of thunderous sounds
that resound through your days,
of glistening lanterns
that brighten your nights;
City, oh, city
of shining delights.

Just for One Day

Hey, sidewalk pacers
bumper riders
long-legged gliders
stalkers, ledge walkers
roof straddlers
fence jumpers
stompers, trouncers
muggers, sluggers
big burly bouncers
alley runners
stabbers, purse grabbers
hurriers, harriers
scared scurriers
all chased and chasers,
please cease for a moment
oh please,
lie down in a heap
and sleep.

Lillian Morrison

The Riveter

This worker is a fearless one,
a daring acrobat,
He creeps across the narrow beams,
As steady as a cat.
He shifts and swings the girders,
While the wind about him blows.
He drives the red-hot rivets,
Though a fly sits on his nose.
Imagine how it feels to work
Up twenty stories high,
Riveting the girders there
That shine against the sky!

Mabel Watts

Gift with the Wrappings Off

Oh, what can you do with a Christmas pup
In a little apartment three flights up?
He prowls.

And whenever the landlord happens by
With a "Rent's due!" gleam in his fishy eye,
He howls!

Or whenever you dress for a hurry date,
With a frantic prayer that you won't be late,
He "helps"!

Or when guests sit down in the rocking chair
And neglect to see if a tail is there.
He yelps;

And if you protest that he isn't hurt
And call him out from beneath your skirt,
He balks.

Or perhaps there's rain, or a two-foot snow,
Or it's three *a.m.*—then he's got to go
For walks!

And the place you pick for his bed at night
Is the one sure place that he doesn't quite
Approve.

Oh, what can you do with a Christmas pup
In a little apartment three flights up?
Move?

Mary Elizabeth Counselman

City, City

I

City, city,
Wrong and bad,
Looms above me
When I'm sad,
Throws its shadow
On my care,
Sheds its poison
In my air,
Pounds me with its
Noisy fist,
Sprays me with its
Sooty mist.
Till, with sadness
On my face,
I wouldn't live
Another place.

II

City, city,
Golden-clad,
Shines around me
When I'm glad,
Lifts me with its
Strength and height,
Fills me with its
Sound and sight,
Takes me to its
Crowded heart,
Holds me so I
Won't depart.
Till, with gladness
On my face,
I wouldn't live
Another place.

Marci Ridlon

Sing a Song of Subways

Sing a song of subways,
Never see the sun;
Four-and-twenty people
In room for one.

When the doors are opened—
Everybody run.

Eve Merriam

Things to Do If You Are a Subway

Pretend you are a dragon.
Live in underground caves.
Roar about underneath the city.
Swallow piles of people.
Spit them out at the next station.
Zoom through the darkness.
Be an express.
Go fast.
Make as much noise as you please.

Bobbi Katz

Flowers Are a Silly Bunch

Flowers are a silly bunch
While trees are sort of bossy.
Lakes are shy
The earth is calm
And rivers do seem saucy.
Hills are good
But mountains mean
While weeds all ask for pity.
I guess the country can be nice
But I prefer the city.

Arnold Spilka

Rudolph Is Tired of the City

These buildings are too close to me.
I'd like to PUSH away.
I'd like to live in the country,
And spread my arms all day.

I'd like to spread my breath out, too—
As farmers' sons and daughters do.

I'd tend the cows and chickens.
I'd do the other chores.
Then, all the hours left I'd go
A-SPREADING out-of-doors.

Gwendolyn Brooks

That May Morning

That May morning—very early—
As I walked the city street,
Not a single store was open
Any customer to greet.

That May morning—it was early—
As I walked the avenue,
I could stop and stare and window-shop,
And hear the pigeons coo.

Early, early that May morning
I could skip and jump and run
And make shadows on the sidewalk,
Not disturbing anyone.

All the windows, all the lamp posts,
Every leaf on every tree
That was growing through the sidewalk
Seemed to be there just for me.

Leland B. Jacobs

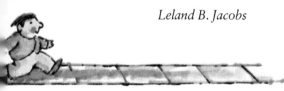

Umbilical

You can take away my mother,
you can take away my sister,
but don't take away
my little transistor.

I can do without sunshine,
I can do without Spring,
but I can't do without
my ear to that thing.

I can live without water,
in a hole in the ground,
but I can't live without
that sound that sound that sound that sOWnd.

Eve Merriam

Zebra

white sun
black
fire escape,

morning
grazing like a zebra
outside my window.

Judith Thurman

The People Upstairs

The people upstairs all practice ballet.
Their living room is a bowling alley.
Their bedroom is full of conducted tours.
Their radio is louder than yours.
They celebrate weekends all the week.
When they take a shower, your ceilings leak.
They try to get their parties to mix
By supplying their guests with Pogo sticks,
And when their orgy at last abates,
They go to the bathroom on roller skates.
I might love the people upstairs wondrous
If instead of above us, they just lived under us.

Ogden Nash

The People

The ants are walking under the ground,
And the pigeons are flying over the steeple,
And in between are the people.

Elizabeth Madox Roberts

Sunrise

The city YAWNS
And rubs its eyes,
Like baking bread
Begins to rise.

Frank Asch

Crowds

Crowds pushing
Into the subway
Scare me.
(Maybe I'll grow out of it.)
Crowds rushing
At the traffic light
Make me wonder.
Crowds
Passing
Dashing
Across the honking streets
Carry me along.
Crowds that stand
In
Long
Lines
Forever
For a ticket,
For a movie,
I don't dig.
Crowds
Slicking
Up and down escalators,
Crowds
Popping out of elevators
Don't turn me on.
(Maybe I'll grow out of it.)

Virginia Schonborg

Concrete Mixers

The drivers are washing the concrete mixers;
Like elephant tenders they hose them down.
Tough gray-skinned monsters standing ponderou
Elephant-bellied and elephant-nosed,
Standing in muck up to their wheel-caps,
Like rows of elephants, tail to trunk.
Their drivers perch on their backs like mahouts,
Sending the sprays of water up.
They rid the trunk-like trough of concrete,
Direct the spray to the bulging sides,
Turn and start the monsters moving.
       Concrete mixers
       Move like elephants
       Bellow like elephants
       Spray like elephants,
Concrete mixers are urban elephants,
Their trunks are raising a city.

Patricia Hubbell

Sing a Song of People

Sing a song of people
   Walking fast or slow;
People in the city,
   Up and down they go.

   People on the sidewalk,
   People on the bus;
   People passing, passing,
   In back and front of us.
   People on the subway
   Underneath the ground;
   People riding taxis
   Round and round and round.

   People with their hats on,
   Going in the doors;
   People with umbrellas
   When it rains and pours.
   People in tall buildings
   And in stores below;
   Riding elevators
   Up and down they go.

   People walking singly,
   People in a crowd;
   People saying nothing,
   People talking loud.
   People laughing, smiling,
   Grumpy people too;
   People who just hurry
   And never look at you!

   Sing a song of people
      Who like to come and go;
   Sing of city people
      You see but never know!

Lois Lenski

Pigeons

Pigeons are city folk
content
to live with concrete
and cement.

They seldom
try
the sky.

A pigeon never sings
of hill
and flowering hedge,
but busily commutes
from sidewalk
to his ledge.

   Oh pigeon, what a waste of wings!

Lilian Moore

They've All Gone South

Redbird, bluebird,
Bird with yellow mouth
All the pretty little birds
Have flown away south,
But the little dusty sparrow
With his wings of rusty brown
For some peculiar reason
Lingers in the town
And little city children
Who wouldn't know a robin
From a cuckoo or a crow
Will hear the little sparrows
Chirping in the snow.

Mary Britton Miller

Stickball

The broomstick bat
Is good.
You've got to be fast,
You've got to dodge.
Stickball's a tough game
In the city.
The ball ricochets
From fender to hood
To stoop—you've got it!
You've got to be fast,
You've got to dodge
In the city.

Virginia Schonborg

A Sad Song About
Greenwich Village

She lives in a garret
    Up a haunted stair,
And even when she's frightened
    There's nobody to care.

She cooks so small a dinner
    She dines on the smell,
And even if she's hungry
    There's nobody to tell.

She sweeps her musty lodging
    As the dawn steals near,
And even when she's crying
    There's nobody to hear.

I haven't seen my neighbor
    Since a long time ago,
And even if she's dead
    There's nobody to know.

Frances Park

Fog

The fog comes
on little cat feet.

It sits looking
over harbor and city
on silent haunches
and then moves on.

Carl Sandburg

Alley Cat School

Do alley cats go
        to alley cat school?
Where they learn how to slink
        and stay out of sight?
Where they learn how to find
        warm and comfortable places,
On a cold wintry night?
Do they learn from teachers and books,
        how to topple a garbage can lid?
Did they all go
        to alley cat school?
Is that what they did?

Frank Asch

Open Hydrant

Water rushes up
and gushes,
cooling summer's sizzle.

In a sudden whoosh
it rushes,
not a little drizzle.

First a hush and down
it crashes,
over curbs it swishes.

Just a luscious waterfall
for
cooling city fishes.

Marci Ridlon

Rainy Nights

I like the town on rainy nights
   When everything is wet—
When all the town has magic lights
   And streets of shining jet!

When all the rain about the town
   Is like a looking-glass,
And all the lights are upside-down
   Below me as I pass.

In all the pools are velvet skies,
   And down the dazzling street
A fairy city gleams and lies
   In beauty at my feet.

Irene Thompson

April Rain Song

Let the rain kiss you.
Let the rain beat upon your head with silver
   liquid drops.
Let the rain sing you a lullaby.

The rain makes still pools on the sidewalk.
The rain makes running pools in the gutter.
The rain plays a little sleep-song on our roof at
   night—

And I love the rain.

Langston Hughes

City Lights

Into the endless dark
The lights of the buildings shine,
Row upon twinkling row,
Line upon glistening line.
Up and up they mount
Till the tallest seems to be
The topmost taper set
On a towering Christmas tree.

Rachel Field

The City Dump

City asleep
City asleep
Papers fly at the garbage he
Refuse dumped and
The sea gulls reap
Grapefruit rinds
And coffee grinds
And apple peels.
The sea gull reels and
The field mouse steals
In for a bite
At the end of night
Of crusts and crumbs
And pits of plums.
The white eggshells
And the green-blue smells
And the gray gull's cry
And the red dawn sky. . . .
City asleep
City asleep
A carnival
On the garbage heap.

Felice Holm

City

In the morning the city
Spreads its wings
Making a song
In stone that sings.

In the evening the city
Goes to bed
Hanging lights
About its head.

Langston Hughes

Frightening

Here it comes!
    huge hulk
    in the darkness
    the long freighter
    blacker than the water
    silent as a ghostship
    stealing by
    slowly
    down the dark river.

Claudia Lewis

Where Are You Now?

When the night begins to fall
And the sky begins to glow
You look up and see the tall
City of light begin to grow—
In rows and little golden squares
The lights come out. First here, then there
Behind the windowpanes as though
A million billion bees had built
Their golden hives and honeycombs
Above you in the air.

Mary Britton Miller

Foghorns

The foghorns moaned
    in the bay last night
    so sad
    so deep
I thought I heard the city
    crying in its sleep.

Lilian Moore

Cockpit in the Clouds

Two thousand feet beneath our wheels
The city sprawls across the land
Like heaps of children's blocks outflung,
In tantrums, by a giant hand.
To east a silver spire soars
And seeks to pierce our lower wing.
Above its grasp we drift along,
A tiny, droning, shiny thing.

The noon crowds pack the narrow streets.
The el trains move so slow, so slow.
Amidst their traffic, chaos, life,
The city's busy millions go.
Up here, aloof, we watch them crawl.
In crystal air we seem to poise
Behind our motor's throaty roar—
Down there, we're just another noise.

Dick Dorrance

CHILDREN, CHILDREN EVERYWHERE

Children, children everywhere,
children dark and children fair,
children of all shapes and sizes,
children springing odd surprises,
children chasing, running races,
children laughing, making faces,
children cooking mud for dinner,
children, every one a winner.

Children jumping, children wiggling,
children grumping, children giggling,
children singing, sneezing, weeping,
children sometimes even sleeping,
children giving children hugs,
children chewing worms and bugs,
children in their parents' hair,
children, children everywhere.

Advice to Small Children

Eat no green apples or you'll droop,
Be careful not to get the croup,
Avoid the chicken-pox and such,
And don't fall out of windows much.

Edward Anthony

Hug O' War

I will not play at tug o' war.
I'd rather play at hug o' war,
Where everyone hugs
Instead of tugs,
Where everyone giggles
And rolls on the rug,
Where everyone kisses,
And everyone grins,
And everyone cuddles,
And everyone wins.

Shel Silverstein

Changing

I know what *I* feel like;
I'd like to be *you*
And feel what *you* feel like
And do what *you* do.
I'd like to change places
For maybe a week
And look like your look-like
And speak as you speak
And think what you're thinking
And go where you go
And feel what you're feeling
And know what you know.
I wish we could do it;
What fun it would be
If I could try you out
And you could try me.

Mary Ann Hoberman

The Joke

The joke you just told isn't funny one bit.
It's pointless and dull, wholly lacking in
    wit.
It's so old and stale, it's beginning to
    smell!
Besides, it's the one I was going to tell.

Anonymous

Somebody

Somebody loves you deep and true.
If I weren't so bashful, I'd tell you who.

Anonymous

I Love You

I love you, I love you,
I love you divine,
Please give me your bubble gum,
You're *sitting* on mine!

Anonymous

Question

Do you love me
Or do you not?
You told me once
But I forgot.

Anonymous

Love

I love you, I like you,
I really do like you.
I do *not* want to strike you,
I do *not* want to shove you.
I *do* want to like you,
I *do* want to love you;
And like you and love you
And love you and love you.

William Jay Smith

Huckleberry, Gooseberry, Raspberry Pie

Huckleberry, gooseberry, raspberry pie
All sweetest things one cannot buy.
Peppermint candies are six for a penny,
But true love & kisses, one cannot buy any.

Clyde Watson

I Saw a Little Girl I Hate

I saw a little girl I hate
And kicked her with my toes.
She turned
And smiled
And KISSED me!
Then she punched me in the nose.

Arnold Spilka

I Hate Harry

I hate Harry like . . . like . . . OOO!
I hate Harry like . . . GEE!
I hate that Harry like—poison.
I hate! hate! hate! HAR-RY!

Rat! Dope! Skunk! Bum! Liar!
Dumber than the dumbest dumb flea!
BOY! . . . do I hate Harry,
I hate him the most that can be.

I hate him a hundred, thousand, million
Doubled, and multiplied by three,
A skillion, trillion, zillion more times
Than Harry, that rat, hates me.

Miriam Chaikin

Double-Barreled Ding-Dong-Bat

Why,
You—

Double-barreled,
Disconnected,
Supersonic
Ding-dong-bat:

Don't you dare come
Near me, or I'll
Disconnect you
Just like that!

Dennis Lee

Puzzle

My best friend's name is Billy
But his best friend is Fred
And Fred's is Willy Wiffleson
And Willy's best is Ted.
Ted's best pal is Samuel
While Samuel's is Paul. . . .
It's funny Paul says I'm his best
I hate him most of all.

Arnold Spilka

John, Tom, and James

John was a bad boy, and beat a poor cat;
Tom put a stone in a blind man's hat;
James was the boy who neglected his prayers;
They've all grown up ugly, and nobody cares.

Charles Henry Ross

There Was a Little Girl

There was a little girl, who had a little curl
   Right in the middle of her forehead,
And when she was good, she was very, very good,
   But when she was bad she was horrid.

Henry Wadsworth Longfellow

Tag Along

Sing song
Tag along
Standing by the wall

Crank pot
Whine a lot
Just because you're small

Big shot
Red hot
Go and wilt a flower

Rough tough
Mean enough
To make the milk turn sour

Nina Payne

Read This with Gestures

It isn't proper, I guess you know,
   To dip your hands—like this—in the snow,
And make a snowball, and look for a hat,
   And try to knock it off—like that!

John Ciardi

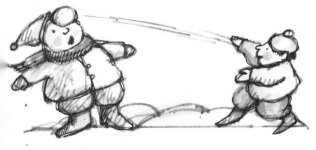

Yip-yap Rattletrap

Yip-yap Rattletrap
Prating noisy Pest
Stuff a Muffin in your Mouth
And let my poor Ears rest!

Clyde Watson

Two People

Two people live in Rosamund,
   And one is very nice;
The other is devoted
   To every kind of vice—

To walking where the puddles are,
   And eating far too quick,
And saying words she shouldn't know,
   And wanting spoons to lick.

Two people live in Rosamund,
   And one (I say it twice)
Is very nice *and* very good:
   The other's only nice.

E. V. Rieu

Ten Kinds

Winnie Whiney, all things grieve her;
Fannie Fibber, who'd believe her?
Lotty Loozem, late to school, sir;
Albert Allplay, quite a fool, sir;
Kitty Kissem, loved by many;
George Grump, not loved by any;
Ralph Ruff—beware his fist, sir;
Tillie Tattle, like a blister;
Gus Goodactin, bright and cheery;
Sammy Selfish, sour and dreary.
Do you know them, as I've sung them?
Easy 'tis to choose among them.

Mary Mapes Dodge

Table Manners

The Goops they lick their fingers,
  And the Goops they lick their knives;
They spill their broth on the tablecloth—
  Oh, they lead disgusting lives!
The Goops they talk while eating,
  And loud and fast they chew;
And that is why I'm glad that I
  Am not a Goop—are you?

Gelett Burgess

Jack

That's Jack;
Lay a stick on his back!
What's he done? I cannot say.
We'll find out tomorrow,
And beat him today.

Charles Henry Ross

Bubble Gum

I'm in trouble
made a bubble
peeled it off my nose

Felt a rock
inside my sock
got gum between my toes

Made another
told my brother
we could blow a pair

Give three cheers
now our ears
are sticking to our hair.

Nina Payne

Why Run?

Jane won't touch a caterpillar,
Mary's frightened of a mouse,
Sally shrieks and runs for Daddy
When a moth flies in the house.
Pam's afraid of shiny beetles,
Spiders make Melinda squirm,
Susan nearly has HYS-TER-ICS
If you chase her with a worm!

Aren't they foolish to be frightened?
Fancy making such a fuss
Over harmless creepy-crawlies
Who are scared to death—of US.

Norah Smaridge

Did You?

Having little kids around, they say, is truly bliss;
But did you ever hear of any little kid like this?

He swallows pits,
Has temper fits,
Spills the ink,
And clogs the sink.
And, oh my gosh!
He hates to wash!
He plays with matches,
And grabs and snatches.
He scrawls on walls,
And sprawls and bawls,
And argues and fights,
And kicks and bites. . . .
You say you never heard of
  any kid like that, you do—
Well, I know one who's
  just like that and it's
          Y
            O
              U!

William Cole

The Story of Augustus Who Would Not Have Any Soup

Augustus was a chubby lad;
Fat ruddy cheeks Augustus had:
And everybody saw with joy
The plump and hearty, healthy boy.
He ate and drank as he was told,
And never let his soup get cold.
But one day, one cold winter's day,
He screamed out "Take the soup away!
O take the nasty soup away!
I won't have any soup today."

Next day, now look, the picture shows
How lank and lean Augustus grows!
Yet, though he feels so weak and ill,
The naughty fellow cries out still
"Not any soup for me, I say:
O take the nasty soup away!
I *won't* have any soup today."

The third day comes: Oh what a sin!
To make himself so pale and thin.
Yet, when the soup is put on table,
He screams, as loud as he is able,
"Not any soup for me, I say:
O take the nasty soup away!
I WON'T have any soup today."

Look at him, now the fourth day's come!
He scarcely weighs a sugar-plum;
He's like a little bit of thread,
And, on the fifth day, he was—dead!

Heinrich Hoffmann

Eat-it-all Elaine

I went away last August
To summer camp in Maine,
And there I met a camper
Called Eat-it-all Elaine.
Although Elaine was quiet,
She liked to cause a stir
By acting out the nickname
Her camp-mates gave to her.

The day of our arrival
At Cabin Number Three
When girls kept coming over
To greet Elaine and me,
She took a piece of Kleenex
And calmly chewed it up,
Then strolled outside the cabin
And ate a buttercup.

Elaine, from that day forward,
Was always in command.
On hikes, she'd eat some birch-bark.
On swims, she'd eat some sand.
At meals, she'd swallow prune-pits
And never have a pain,
While everyone around her
Would giggle, "Oh, Elaine!"

One morning, berry-picking,
A bug was in her pail,
And though we thought for certain
Her appetite would fail,
Elaine said, "Hmm, a stinkbug."
And while we murmured, "Ooh,"
She ate her pail of berries
And ate the stinkbug, too.

The night of Final Banquet
When counselors were handing
Awards to different children
Whom they believed outstanding,
To every *thinking* person
At summer camp in Maine
The Most Outstanding Camper
Was Eat-it-all Elaine.

Kaye Starbird

Tired Tim

Poor tired Tim! It's sad for him
He lags the long bright morning through,
Ever so tired of nothing to do;
He moons and mopes the livelong day,
Nothing to think about, nothing to say;
Up to bed with his candle to creep,
Too tired to yawn, too tired to sleep:
Poor tired Tim! It's sad for him.

Walter de la Mare

Wendy in Winter

No wonder Wendy's coat blew off.
She didn't have it zipped.
And—since she didn't watch for slush—
No wonder Wendy slipped.
No wonder Wendy froze her feet
Although her boots were lined,
Because when Wendy left for school
She left her boots behind.
And since she didn't dodge the ice
That sagged an apple bough,
No wonder Wendy's hatless head
Has seven stitches now.

Kaye Starbird

Queenie

Queenie's strong and Queenie's tall.
You should see her bat a ball,
Ride a bike, or climb a wall.
(Queenie's not her name at all.)

Queenie's nimble, Queenie's quick.
You should see her throw a stick,
Watch her saw a board that's thick,
See her do her tumbling trick.

Queenie's not afraid, like me,
Of snakes or climbing up a tree.
(I think that's why the boys agree,
Queenie's what her name should be.)

Leland B. Jacobs

Fernando

Fernando has a basketball.
He tap, tap, taps it down the hall,
then leaps up high and shoots with care.
The fact a basket isn't there,
he totally dismisses.
He says he never misses.
My crazy friend Fernando.

Marci Ridlon

Tony Baloney

Tony Baloney is fibbing again—
Look at him wiggle and try to pretend.
Tony Baloney is telling a lie:
Phony old Tony Baloney, goodbye!

Dennis Lee

110

Follow the Leader

Whatever he does, you have to do too,
because he is the leader.
When he jumps off the porch, you have to jump too
(even when you're a little bit scared),
because he is the leader.
If he yells "blueberry" very loud
or says "Hello" to a frog,
you have to do all those things
because he is the leader.

But then his turn is over.
And you are next.
And everyone stands behind you
and waits for you to begin
and they have to do whatever silly things
you can think of
because YOU are the leader now.

Kathleen Fraser

Jessica Jane

Jessica Jane is the kind of cook
Who doesn't need a recipe book.
Little trouble indeed she takes
When she makes puddings and pies and cakes.
With a twist of her wrist and a pat-a-pat
She turns them out in a row—like that!
There in a row in the summer sun
They bake and bake till they're all well done.
Grocery problems are not for her—
She has plenty of mud and a stick to stir.

May Justus

Freddy

Here is the story
Of Freddy, my friend,
Who ran out in the traffic,
And that is the end.

Dennis Lee

Girls Can, Too!

Tony said: "Boys are better!
  They can . . .

    whack a ball,
    ride a bike with one hand
    leap off a wall."

I just listened
  and when he was through,
I laughed and said:

    "Oh, yeah! Well, girls can, too!"

Then I leaped off the wall,
  and rode away
With *his* 200 baseball cards
  I won that day.

Lee Bennet Hopkins

Little Clotilda

Little Clotilda,
Well and hearty,
Thought she'd like
To give a party.
But as her friends
Were shy and wary,
Nobody came
But her own canary.

Anonymous

We're Racing, Racing down the Walk

We're racing, racing down the walk,
Over the pavement and round the block.
We rumble along till the sidewalk ends—
Felicia and I and half our friends.
Our hair flies backward. It's whish and whirr!
She roars at me and I shout at her
As past the porches and garden gates
We rattle and rock
On our roller skates.

Phyllis McGinley

No Girls Allowed

When we're playing tag
and the girls want to play,
we yell and we scream
and we chase them away.

When we're playing stickball
or racing our toys
and the girls ask to join,
we say, "Only for boys."

We play hide-and-go-seek
and the girls wander near.
They say, "Please let us hide."
We pretend not to hear.

We don't care for girls
so we don't let them in,
we think that they're dumb—
and besides, they might win.

Jack Prelutsky

maggie and milly and molly and may

maggie and millie and molly and may
went down to the beach(to play one day)

and maggie discovered a shell that sang
so sweetly she couldn't remember her troubles,and

milly befriended a stranded star
whose rays five languid fingers were;

and molly was chased by a horrible thing
which raced sideways while blowing bubbles:and

may came home with a smooth round stone
as small as a world and as large as alone.

For whatever we lost(like a you or a me)
it's always ourselves we find in the sea

e. e. cummings

Wrestling

I like wrestling with Herbie because
he's my best friend.
We poke each other
(but not very hard)
and punch each other
(but not very hard)
and roll on the grass
and pretend to have fights
just to make our sisters scream.
But sometimes if he hits me too much
and it hurts,
I get mad
and I punch him back
as hard as I can
and then we both are crying
and going into our houses
and slamming our back doors on each other.
But the next day, if it's sunny,
we come out into our yards
and grin at each other,
and sometimes he gives me an apple
or I give him a cookie and
then we start wrestling again.

Kathleen Fraser

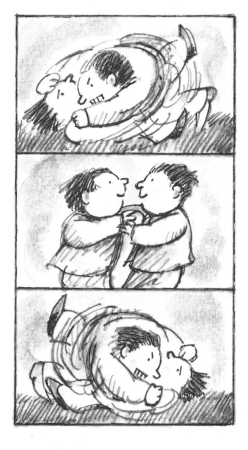

Measles

The few times back in the early fall
When kids had measles
And stayed home sick,
Our classroom teacher would have us all
Writing them letters
To get well quick.

But now, when most of the kids in school
Are out with measles
They somehow catch,
Our teacher's suddenly changed her rule
And just ignores them
And lets them scratch.

She says that lately we all get measle-y
Much too easily.

Kaye Starbird

Wiggly Giggles

I've got the wiggly-wiggles today,
And I just can't sit still.
My teacher says she'll have to find
A stop-me-wiggle pill.

I've got the giggly-giggles today;
I couldn't tell you why.
But if Mary hiccups one more time
I'll giggle till I cry.

I've got to stamp my wiggles out
And hold my giggles in,
Cause wiggling makes me giggle
And gigglers never win.

*Stacy Jo Crossen
and Natalie Anne Covell*

Barbershop

When you visit the barber
    And sit in his chair,
Don't squirm
Like a worm
    While he's cutting your hair.

Don't shiver
And quiver
    And bounce up and down.
Don't shuffle
And snuffle
    And act like a clown.

Each wiggle
Will jiggle
    The blades of the shears.
Clip-clip,
Clip-clip.
Those scissors can slip
And snip
Off a tip
    Of one of your tender pink ears!

Martin Gardner

Since Hanna Moved Away

The tires on my bike are flat.
The sky is grouchy gray.
At least it sure feels like that
Since Hanna moved away.

Chocolate ice cream tastes like
prunes.
December's come to stay.
They've taken back the Mays and
Junes
Since Hanna moved away.

Flowers smell like halibut.
Velvet feels like hay.
Every handsome dog's a mutt
Since Hanna moved away.

Nothing's fun to laugh about.
Nothing's fun to play.
They call me, but I won't come
out
Since Hanna moved away.

Judith Viorst

A Lullaby

Speak roughly to your little boy,
    And beat him when he sneezes:
He only does it to annoy,
    Because he knows it teases.

    Wow! wow! wow!

I speak severely to my boy,
    I beat him when he sneezes;
For he can thoroughly enjoy
    The pepper when he pleases!

    Wow! wow! wow!

Lewis Carroll

What in the World?

What in the world
    goes whiskery friskery
        meowling and prowling
            napping and lapping
                at silky milk?
Psst,
What is it?

What in the world
    goes leaping and beeping
        onto a lily pad onto a log
            onto a tree stump or down to the bog?
Splash, blurp,
Kerchurp!

What in the World
    goes gnawing and pawing
        scratching and latching
            sniffing and squiffing
                nibbling for tidbits of leftover cheese?
Please?

What in the world
    jumps with a hop and a bump
        and a tail that can thump
            has pink pointy ears and a twitchy nose
                looking for anything crunchy that grows?
A carroty lettucey cabbagey luncheon
To munch on?

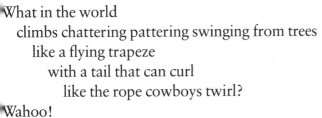

What in the world
   climbs chattering pattering swinging from trees
     like a flying trapeze
      with a tail that can curl
       like the rope cowboys twirl?
Wahoo!
Here's a banana for you!

     What in the world
      goes stalking and balking
       running and sunning
        thumping and dumping
         lugging and hugging
          swinging and singing
           wriggling and giggling
           sliding and hiding
            throwing and knowing and
            growing and growing
           much too big for
            last year's clothes?
  Who knows?

Eve Merriam

ME I AM!

I am the only ME I AM
who qualifies as me;
no ME I AM has been before,
and none will ever be.

No other ME I AM can feel
the feelings I've within;
no other ME I AM can fit
precisely in my skin.

There is no other ME I AM
who thinks the thoughts I do;
the world contains one ME I AM,
there is no room for two.

I am the only ME I AM
this earth shall ever see;
that ME I AM I always am
is no one else but ME!

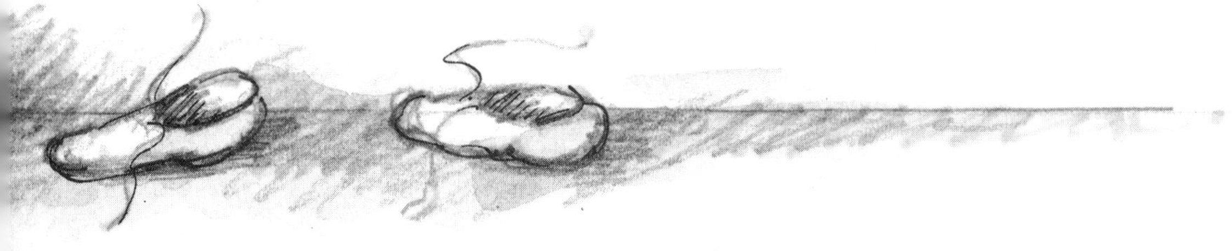

Me

As long as I live
I shall always be
My Self—and no other,
Just me.

Like a tree—
Willow, elder,
Aspen, thorn,
Or cypress forlorn.

Like a flower,
For its hour—

Primrose, or pink,
Or a violet—
Sunned by the sun,
And with dewdrops wet.

Always just me.
Till the day come on
When I leave this body,
It's all then done,
And the spirit within it
Is gone.

Walter de la Mare

My Name Is . . .

My name is Sluggery-wuggery
My name is Worms-for-tea
My name is Swallow-the-table-leg
My name is Drink-the-Sea.

My name is I-eat-saucepans
My name is I-like-snails
My name is Grand-piano-George
My name is I-ride-whales.

My name is Jump-the-chimney
My name is Bite-my-knee
My name is Jiggery-pokery
And Riddle-me-ree, and ME.

Pauline Clarke

My Father Owns the Butcher Shop

My father owns the butcher shop,
My mother cuts the meat,
And I'm the little hot dog
That runs around the street.

Anonymous

I Am Rose

I am Rose my eyes are blue
I am Rose and who are you
I am Rose and when I sing
I am Rose like anything.

Gertrude Stein

The Reason I Like Chocolate

The reason I like chocolate
is I can lick my fingers
and nobody tells me I'm not polite

I especially like scary movies
'cause I can snuggle with Mommy
or my big sister and they don't laugh

I like to cry sometimes 'cause
everybody says "what's the matter
don't cry"

and I like books
for all those reasons
but mostly 'cause they just make me
happy

and I really like
to be happy

Nikki Giovanni

Every Time I Climb a Tree

Every time I climb a tree
Every time I climb a tree
Every time I climb a tree
I scrape a leg
Or skin a knee
And every time I climb a tree
I find some ants
Or dodge a bee
And get the ants
All over me

And every time I climb a tree
Where have you been?
They say to me
But don't they know that I am free
Every time I climb a tree?
I like it best
To spot a nest
That has an egg
Or maybe three

And then I skin
The other leg
But every time I climb a tree
I see a lot of things to see
Swallows rooftops and TV
And all the fields and farms there be
Every time I climb a tree
Though climbing may be good for ants
It isn't awfully good for pants
But still it's pretty good for me
Every time I climb a tree

David McCord

Me

"My nose is blue,
My teeth are green,
My face is like a soup tureen.
I look just like a lima bean.
I'm very, very lovely.
My feet are far too short
And long.
My hands are left and right
And wrong.
My voice is like the hippo's song.
I'm very, very,
Very, very,
Very, very
Lovely?"

Karla Kuskin

Mark's Fingers

I like my fingers.
They grip a ball,
Turn a page,
Break a fall,
Help whistle
A call.
Shake hands
And shoot
Rubber bands.
When candy is offered
They take enough.
They fill my pockets
With wonderful stuff,
And they always tell me
Smooth from rough.
They follow rivers
On a map,
They double over
When I rap,
They smack together
When I clap.
They button buttons,
Tie shoelaces,
Open doors to
Brand-new places.
They shape and float
My paper ships,
Fasten papers to
Paper clips,
And carry ice cream
To my lips. . . .

Mary O'Neill

When I Was Lost

Underneath my belt
My stomach was a stone.
Sinking was the way I felt.
And hollow.
And Alone.

Dorothy Aldis

Keziah

I have a secret place to go.
Not anyone may know.

And sometimes when the wind is rough
I cannot get there fast enough.

And sometimes when my mother
Is scolding my big brother,

My secret place, it seems to me,
Is quite the only place to be.

Gwendolyn Brooks

Just Me

Nobody sees what I can see,
For back of my eyes there is only me.
And nobody knows how my thoughts begin,
For there's only myself inside my skin.
Isn't it strange how everyone owns
Just enough skin to cover his bones?
My father's would be too big to fit—
I'd be all wrinkled inside of it.
And my baby brother's is much too small—
It just wouldn't cover me up at all.
But I feel just right in the skin *I* wear,
And there's nobody like me anywhere.

Margaret Hillert

If No One Ever Marries Me

If no one ever marries me—
And I don't see why they should;
For nurse says I'm not pretty,
And I'm seldom very good—

If no one ever marries me
I shan't mind very much;
I shall buy a squirrel in a cage,
And a little rabbit hutch.

I shall have a cottage near a wood,
And a pony all my own.
And a little lamb quite clean and tame
That I can take to town.

And when I'm getting really old,
At twenty-eight or nine,
I shall buy a little orphan girl
And bring her up as mine.

Laurence Alma-Tadema

How to Get There

I go
through Sunday's tunnel, hushed and deep;
up Monday's mountain, craggy and steep;
along Tuesday's trail, winding and slow;
into Wednesday's woods, still halfway to go;
over Thursday's bridge, shaky and tall;
through the hidden gate in Friday's wall
to get to
SATURDAY.

I wish there were a shorter way.

Bonnie Nims

A Wolf . . .

A wolf
I considered myself
but
the owls are hooting
and
the night I fear.

Osage Indian

Sulk

I scuff
    my feet along
And puff
    my lower lip
I sip my milk
    in slurps
And huff
And frown
And stamp around
And tip my chair
    back from the table
Nearly fall down
    but I don't care
I scuff
And puff
And frown
And huff
And stamp
And pout
Till I forget
What it's about

Felice Holman

Dust of Snow

The way a crow
Shook down on me
The dust of snow
From a hemlock tree
Has given my heart
A change of mood,
And saved some part
of a day I rued.

Robert Frost

Broom Balancing

Millicent can play the flute
and Francine can dance a jig,
but I can balance a broom.

Susanna knows how to bake cookies
and Harold can stand on one foot
but I can balance a broom.

Jeffry can climb a ladder backwards
and Andrew can count to five thousand and two,
but I can balance a broom.

Do you think a circus might discover me?

Kathleen Fraser

About Feet

The centipede is not complete
Unless he has one hundred feet.
Spiders must have eight for speed,
And six is what all insects need.
Other creatures by the score
Cannot do with less than four.
But two are quite enough, you know,
To take me where I want to go.

Margaret Hillert

The Sidewalk Racer
OR
ON THE SKATEBOARD

Skimming
an asphalt sea
I swerve, I curve, I
sway; I speed to whirring
sound an inch above the
ground; I'm the sailor
and the sail, I'm the
driver and the wheel
I'm the one and only
single engine
human auto
mobile.

Lillian Morrison

Basketball Star

When I get big
I want to be the best
basketball player in the world.
I'll make jumpshots, hookballs
and layups
and talk about dribble—
mine'll be outta sight!

Karama Fufuka

basketball

when spanky goes
to the playground all the big boys say
    hey big time—what's happenin'
'cause his big brother plays basketball for their high school
and he gives them the power sign and says
    you got it
but when i go and say
    what's the word
they just say
    your nose is running junior

one day i'll be seven feet tall
even if i never get a big brother
and i'll stuff that sweaty ball down
their laughing throats

Nikki Giovanni

I Can Fly

I can fly, of course,
Very low,
Not fast,
Rather slow.
I spread my arms
Like wings,
Lean on the wind,
And my body zings
About.
Nothing showy—
A few loops
And turns—
But for the most
Part,
I just coast.

However,
Since people are prone
To talk about
It,
I generally prefer,
Unless I am alone,
Just to walk about.

Felice Holman

Song

I'd much rather sit there in the sun
watching the snow drip from the trees
and the milkman's footsteps fill up with water
and the shadow of the spruce tree branches waving
over the sparkle on the leftover snow
and the water dripping in front of my eyes
and the water dripping from the roof
from the bushes of sparkle the water is dripping
the water is dripping from my eyes it is not dripping
I'd much rather sit in the sun the sun
I'd much rather sit in the sun
listening to the shovels scraping
and the birds that whistle on the wires that are dripping
and the backporch is shining
the steam is floating up
the steam floats up around me like my breathing was be
and the maple tree is gleaming in the branches that are b
above the backporch that is steaming
and I take off my shoes
I take off my stockings and
I sit in the sun I am sitting in the sun
I'd much rather sit here in the sun

Ruth Kra

Growing Up

When I was seven
We went for a picnic
Up to a magic
Foresty place.
I knew there were tigers
Behind every boulder,
Though I didn't meet one
Face to face.

When I was older
We went for a picnic
Up to the very same
Place as before,
And all of the trees
And the rocks were so little
They couldn't hide tigers
Or *me* anymore.

Harry Behn

Stupid Old Myself

Stupid old myself today
Found a four-leaf clover,
Left it where it blew away,
All my good luck's over.
Done and finished, gone astray
Stupid old myself today.

Stupid with a brand-new kite
Lost it in a tree
Way up high and tangled tight—
No more kite for me.

Stupid falling off a log
When I tried to get
Close enough to catch a frog
Came home very wet.

Then I swapped my teddy bear
In a stupid muddle
For a doll that's lost her hair.
No more bear to cuddle.

Walking slowly and alone
Stupid and in sorrow
I just found a lucky stone—
Maybe I'll be smart tomorrow.
With today one day behind me
Maybe my good luck will find me.

Russell Hoban

Everybody Says

Everybody says
I look just like my mother.
Everybody says
I'm the image of Aunt Bee.
Everybody says
My nose is like my father's
But *I* want to look like *ME*!

Dorothy Aldis

The Marrog

My desk's at the back of the class
    And nobody, nobody knows
        I'm a Marrog from Mars
With a body of brass
    And seventeen fingers and toes.

Wouldn't they shriek if they knew
    I've three eyes at the back of my head
        And my hair is bright purple
My nose is deep blue
    And my teeth are half-yellow, half-red.

My five arms are silver, and spiked
    With knives on them sharper than spears.
I could go back right now if I liked—
    And return in a million light-years.

I could gobble them all
For I'm seven foot tall
    And I'm breathing green flames from my ears.

Wouldn't they yell if they knew,
    If they guessed that a Marrog was here?
Ha-ha, they haven't a clue—
    Or wouldn't they tremble with fear!
"Look, look, a Marrog"
    They'd all scream—and SMACK
The blackboard would fall and the ceiling would crack
    And teacher would faint, I suppose.
But I grin to myself, sitting right at the back
    And nobody, nobody knows.

R. C. Scriven

Surprises

Surprises are round
 Or long and tallish.
Surprises are square
 Or flat and smallish.

Surprises are wrapped
 With paper and bow,
And hidden in closets
 Where secrets won't show.

Surprises are often
 Good things to eat;
A get-well toy or
 A birthday treat.

Surprises come
 In such interesting sizes—
I LIKE
 SURPRISES!

Jean Conder Soule

Don't Tell Me That I Talk Too Much!

Don't tell me that I talk too much!
Don't say it!
Don't you dare!
I only say important things
Like why it's raining where.
Or when or how or why or what
Might happen here or there.
And why a thing is this or that
And who is bound to care.
So don't tell me I talk too much!
Don't say it!
DON'T YOU DARE!

Arnold Spilka

If We Didn't Have Birthdays

If we didn't have birthdays, you wouldn't be you.
If you'd never been born, well then what would you do?
If you'd never been born, well then what would you be?
You *might* be a fish! Or a toad in a tree!
You might be a doorknob! Or three baked potatoes!
You might be a bag full of hard green tomatoes.
Or worse than all that . . . Why, you might be a WASN'
A Wasn't has no fun at all. No, he doesn't.
A Wasn't just isn't. He just isn't present.
But you . . . You ARE YOU! And, now isn't that pleasan

Dr. Seuss

History

And I'm thinking how to get out
Of this stuffy room
With its big blackboards.

And I'm trying not to listen
In this boring room
To the way things *were*.

And I'm thinking about later,
Running from the room
Back into the world,

And what the guys will say when
I'm up to bat and hit
A big fat home run.

Myra Cohn Livingston

I'm Really Not Lazy

I'm really not lazy—
I'm not!
I'm not!
It's just that I'm thinking
And thinking
And thinking
A lot!
It's true I don't work
But I can't!
I just can't!
When I'm thinking
And thinking
And thinking
A lot!

Arnold Spilka

I Am Cherry Alive

"I am cherry alive," the little girl sang,
"Each morning I am something new:
I am apple, I am plum, I am just as excited
As the boys who made the Hallowe'en bang:
I am tree, I am cat, I am blossom too:
When I like, if I like, I can be someone new,
Someone very old, a witch in a zoo:
I can be someone else whenever I think who,
And I want to be everything sometimes too:
And the peach has a pit and I know that too,
And I put it in along with everything
To make the grown-ups laugh whenever I sing:
And I sing: *It is true; It is untrue;*
I know, I know, the true is untrue,
The peach has a pit,
The pit has a peach:
And both may be wrong
When I sing my song,
But I don't tell the grown-ups: because it is sad,
And I want them to laugh just like I do
Because they grew up
And forgot what they knew
And they are sure
I will forget it some day too.
They are wrong. They are wrong.
When I sang my song, I knew, I knew!
I am red, I am gold,
I am green, I am blue,
I will always be me,
I will always be new!"

Delmore Schwartz

Winter Clothes

Under my hood I have a hat
And under that
My hair is flat.
Under my coat
My sweater's blue.
My sweater's red.
I'm wearing two.
My muffler muffles to my chin
And round my neck
And then tucks in.
My gloves were knitted
By my aunts.
I've mittens too
And pants
And pants
And boots
And shoes
With socks inside.
The boots are rubber, red and wide.
And when I walk
I must not fall
Because I can't get up at all.

Karla Kuskin

I'm Nobody! Who Are You?

I'm nobody! Who are you?
Are you nobody, too?
Then there's a pair of us—don't tell!
They'd banish us, you know.

How dreary to be somebody!
How public, like a frog,
To tell your name the livelong day
To an admiring bog!

Emily Dickinson

Yawning

Sometimes—I'm sorry—but sometimes,
Sometimes, yes, sometimes I'm bored.
It may be because I'm an idiot;
It may be because I'm floored;

It may be because it is raining,
It may be because it is hot,
It may be because I have eaten
Too much, or because I have not.

But sometimes I *cannot* help yawning
(I'm sorry!) the whole morning through—
And when Teacher's turning her back on us,
It may be that she's yawning too.

Eleanor Farjeon

Rhinos Purple, Hippos Green

My sister says
I shouldn't color
Rhinos purple,
Hippos green.
She says
I shouldn't be so stupid;
Those are things
She's never seen.
But I don't care
What my sister says,
I don't care
What my sister's seen.
I will color
What I want to—
Rhinos purple,
Hippos green.

Michael Patrick Hearn

One Day When We Went Walking

One day when we went walking,
    I found a dragon's tooth,
    A dreadful dragon's tooth.
    "A locust thorn," said Ruth.

One day when we went walking,
    I found a brownie's shoe,
    A brownie's button shoe.
    "A dry pea pod," said Sue.

One day when we went walking,
    I found a mermaid's fan,
    A merry mermaid's fan.
    "A scallop shell," said Dan.

One day when we went walking,
    I found a fairy's dress,
    A fairy's flannel dress.
    "A mullein leaf," said Bess.

Next time that I go walking—
    Unless I meet an elf,
    A funny, friendly elf—
    I'm going by myself!

Valine Hobbs

HOME! YOU'RE WHERE IT'S WARM INSIDE

Home! You are a special place;
you're where I wake and wash my face,
brush my teeth and comb my hair,
change my socks and underwear,
clean my ears and blow my nose,
try on all my parents' clothes.

Home! You're where it's warm inside,
where my tears are gently dried,
where I'm comforted and fed,
where I'm forced to go to bed,
where there's always love to spare;
Home! I'm glad that you are there.

The Wrong Start

I got up this morning and meant to be good,
But things didn't happen the way that they should.

> I lost my toothbrush,
>   I slammed the door,
> I dropped an egg
>   On the kitchen floor,
> I spilled some sugar
>   And after that
> I tried to hurry
>   And tripped on the cat.

Things may get better. I don't know when.
I think I'll go back and start over again.

Marchette Chute

Mother's Nerves

My mother said, "If just once more
I hear you slam that old screen door,
I'll tear out my hair! I'll dive in the stove!"
I gave it a bang and in she dove.

X. J. Kennedy

John

John could take his clothes off
but could not put them on.

His patient mother dressed him,
and said to little John,

"Now, John! You keep your things o
But John had long since gone—

and left a trail of sneakers
and small things in the sun,

so she would know to find him
wherever he might run.

And at the end of every trail
stood Mrs. Jones & Son,

she with all his little clothes,
and little John—with none!

For John could take his clothes off
but could not put them on.

His patient mother dressed him
and on went little John—
and on—
    and on—
        and on—

N. M. Bodecke

Waking

My secret way of waking
is like a place
to hide.
I'm very still,
my eyes are shut.
They all think I am sleeping
but
I'm wide awake inside.

They all think I am sleeping
but
I'm wiggling my toes.
I feel sun-fingers
on my cheek.
I hear voices whisper-speak.
I squeeze my eyes
to keep them shut
so they will think I'm sleeping
BUT
I'm really wide awake inside
—and no one knows!

Lilian Moore

Mother Doesn't Want a Dog

Mother doesn't want a dog.
Mother says they smell,
And never sit when you say sit,
Or even when you yell.
And when you come home late at night
And there is ice and snow,
You have to go back out because
The dumb dog has to go.

Mother doesn't want a dog.
Mother says they shed,
And always let the strangers in
And bark at friends instead,
And do disgraceful things on rugs,
And track mud on the floor,
And flop upon your bed at night
And snore their doggy snore.

Mother doesn't want a dog.
She's making a mistake.
Because, more than a dog, I think
She will not want this snake.

Judith Viorst

Amelia Mixed the Mustard

Amelia mixed the mustard,
    She mixed it good and thick;
She put it in the custard
    And made her Mother sick,
And showing satisfaction
    By many a loud huzza
"Observe," said she, "the action
    Of mustard on Mamma."

A. E. Housman

134

I Wish I Could Meet the Man That Knows

I wish I could meet the man that knows
Who put the fly on my daddy's nose
When my daddy was taking a nap today.
I tried to slap that fly away
So Daddy could sleep. But just as my hand
Came down to slap him, the fly jumped, AND

I hit with a bang—where do you suppose?—
SMACK ON THE END OF DADDY'S
          NOSE!

"Ow!" cried Daddy, and up he jumped.
He jumped so hard that he THUMP-
          BUMPED
His head on the wall.
                    Well, I tried to say,
"See, Daddy, I slapped the fly away."
And I should think he would have thanked me.
But what do you think he did? He
          SPANKED me!

"I was just trying to help!" I said.
But Daddy was looking very red.
"For trying to help, I have to thank you.
But for that smack on the nose, I'll spank
          you!"
And up in the air went his great big hand
As he said, "I hope you understand
It's my nose I'm spanking for, not the fly.
For the fly I thank you."

          And that is why
I wish I could meet the man that knows
Who put the fly on my daddy's nose.
For when I find him, I want to thank him.
And as I do, I want to spank him.

John Ciardi

Some Things Don't Make Any Sense at All

My mom says I'm her sugarplum.
My mom says I'm her lamb.
My mom says I'm completely perfect
Just the way I am.
My mom says I'm a super-special wonderful terrific
        little guy.
My mom just had another baby.
Why?

Judith Viorst

Bringing Up Babies

If babies could speak they'd tell mother or nurse
That slapping was pointless, and why:
For if you're not crying it prompts you to cry,
And if you are—then you cry worse.

Roy Fuller

The First Tooth

Through the house what busy joy,
Just because the infant boy
Has a tiny tooth to show!
I have got a double row,
All as white, and all as small;
Yet no one cares for mine at all.
He can say but half a word,
Yet that single sound's preferred
To all the words that I can say
In the longest summer day.
He cannot walk, yet if he put
With mimic motion out his foot,
As if he thought he were advancing,
It's prized more than my best dancing.

Charles and Mary Lamb

Six Weeks Old

He is so small, he does not know
The summer sun, the winter snow;
The spring that ebbs and comes again,
All this is far beyond his ken.

A little world he feels and sees:
His mother's arms, his mother's knees;
He hides his face against her breast,
And does not care to learn the rest.

Christopher Morley

My Brother

My brother's worth about two cents,
As far as I can see.
I simply cannot understand
Why they would want a "he."

He spends a good part of his day
Asleep inside the crib,
And when he eats, he has to wear
A stupid baby bib.

He cannot walk and cannot talk
And cannot throw a ball.
In fact, he can't do anything—
He's just no fun at all.

It would have been more sensible,
As far as I can see,
Instead of getting one like him
To get one just like me.

Marci Ridlon

Help!

Firemen, firemen!
State police!
Victor's locked in Pop's valise!
Robert's eating kitty litter!
Doctor!
    Lawyer!
        Baby-sitter!

X. J. Kennedy

Lil' Bro'

I have to take my little brother
everywhere I go
'cause I'm his big sister
and Mama told me to.

His nose is always snotty
and his shoes come all untied,
his diapers get wet and dirty,
and he sure does like to cry.

He gets in the dirt
and runs in the street
and doesn't like to mind—
but he's my little brother
and I keep him all the time.

Karama Fufuka

Leave Me Alone

Loving care!
Too much to bear.
Leave me alone!

    Don't brush my hair,
    Don't pat my head,
    Don't tuck me in
    Tonight in bed,
    Don't ask me if I want a sweet,
    Don't fix my favorite things to eat,
    Don't give me lots of good advice.
    And most of all just don't be nice.

But when I've wallowed well in sorrow,
Be nice to me again tomorrow.

Felice Holman

The Myra Song

Myra, Myra, sing-song.
  Myra, Myra, gay.
Myra, Myra, skip-along
  Sings all day.

Myra, Myra, gloom-pout.
  Myra, Myra, sad.
Myra, Myra, poke-about,
  Don't feel bad.

Myra, Myra, chatterbox.
  Myra, Myra, busy.
What a clatter Myra talks!
  Makes me dizzy!

Myra, Myra, la-de-da,
  Dressed in Mummy's clothes,
Playing Lady Fa-la-la,
  Looking down her nose.

Myra, Myra, sleepyhead.
  Myra, Myra, tiny.
Myra, Myra, slugabed.
  The nose I kiss is shiny.

Gay-sad-twinkle-star
  Big-Myra-small.
What a *lot* of her there are!
  I love them all.

John Ciardi

Let Others Share

Let others share your toys, my son,
Do not insist on *all* the fun.
For if you do it's certain that
You'll grow to be an adult brat.

Edward Anthony

In the Motel

Bouncing! bouncing! on the beds
My brother Bob and I cracked heads—

People next door heard the crack,
Whammed on the wall, so we whammed right back.

Dad's razor caused an overload
And wow! did the TV set explode!

Someone's car backed fast and—tinkle!
In our windshield was a wrinkle.

Eight more days on the road? Hooray!
What a bang-up holiday!

X. J. Kennedy

Rules

Do not jump on ancient uncles.

*

Do not yell at average mice.

*

Do not wear a broom to breakfast.

*

Do not ask a snake's advice.

*

Do not bathe in chocolate pudding.

*

Do not talk to bearded bears.

*

Do not smoke cigars on sofas.

*

Do not dance on velvet chairs.

*

Do not take a whale to visit
Russell's mother's cousin's yacht.

*

And whatever else you do do
It is better you
Do not.

Karla Kuskin

The Runaway

I made peanut butter sandwiches.
I didn't leave a mess.
I packed my shell collection
and my velvet party dress,
the locket Grandma gave me
and two pairs of extra socks,
my brother's boy scout flashlight
and some magic wishing rocks.

Oh, they'll be so sorry.
Oh, they'll be so sad,
when they start to realize
what a nifty kid they had.

I'd really like to be here
when they wring their hands and say,
"We drove the poor child to it.
She finally ran away."

If I peeked through the window
I'd see them dressed in black,
and hear them sob and softly sigh,
"Come back, dear child! Come back!"

The house will be so quiet.
My room will be so clean.
And they'll be oh so sorry
that they were oh so mean!

Bobbi Katz

Soap

Just look at those hands!
Did you actually think
That the dirt would come off, my daughter,
By wiggling your fingers
Around in the sink
And slapping the top of the water?

Just look at your face!
Did you really suppose
Those smudges would all disappear
With a dab at your chin
And the tip of your nose
And a rub on the back of one ear?

You tell me your face
And your fingers are *clean*?
Do you think your old Dad is a dope?
Let's try it again
With a different routine.
This time we'll make use of the soap!

Martin Gardner

They're Calling

They're calling, "Nan,
Come at once."
But I don't answer.
   It's not that I don't hear,
   I'm very sharp of ear,
But I'm not Nan,
I'm a dancer.

They're calling, "Nan,
Go and wash."
But I don't go yet.
   Their voices are quite clear,
   I'm humming but I hear,
But I'm not Nan,
I'm a poet.

They're calling, "Nan,
Come to dinner!"
And I stop humming.
   I seem to hear them clearer,
   Now that dinner's nearer.
Well, just for now I'm Nan,
And I say, "Coming."

Felice Holman

What Someone Said When He Was Spanked on the Day Before His Birthday

Some day
I may
Pack my bag and run away.
Some day
I may.
—But not today.

Some night
I might
Slip away in the moonlight.
I might.
Some night.
—But not tonight.

Some night.
Some day.
I might.
I may.
—But right now I think I'll stay.

John Ciardi

Up in the Pine

I'm by myself
I want to be
I don't want anyone
Playing with me

I'm all alone
In the top of the pine
Daddy spanked me
And I don't feel fine

I can look way out
On the woods and lakes
I can hear the buzz
That the chain saw makes

And a woodpecker chopping
In the crabapple tree
With his red crest bobbing
But he doesn't see me

If anybody hollers
I'll pretend I'm not there
I may miss dinner
But I don't care

The pine needles swish
And the wind whistles free
And up in the pine
Is only me

It's starting to rain
But the tree keeps me dry
We toss in the black clouds
The tree and I

Now Daddy's calling.
He never *stays* mad.
He probably feels awful
Because I'm sad.

I'll answer Daddy.
He's concerned about the weather.
I'll climb down and he'll take my hand
And we'll go in the house together.

Nancy Dingman Watson

Going Up

Space-Suit Sammy,
Head in glass,
Watches all
The Martians pass.

Ray gun ready,
Tank in tow,
Rocket waiting—
Systems go!

Whish! by moon,
Over stars,
Past the glint
Of alien cars,

Space-Suit Sammy
At the helm
Knows atomic
Void and realm,

Knows the course,
The way ahead,
Up and up—
And so to bed.

John Travers Moore

Homework

Homework sits on top of Sunday, squashing Sunday flat.
Homework has the smell of Monday, homework's very fat.
Heavy books and piles of paper, answers I don't know.
Sunday evening's almost finished, now I'm going to go
Do my homework in the kitchen. Maybe just a snack,
Then I'll sit right down and start as soon as I run back
For some chocolate sandwich cookies. Then I'll really do
All that homework in a minute. First I'll see what new
Show they've got on television in the living room.
Everybody's laughing there, but misery and gloom
And a full refrigerator are where I am at.
I'll just have another sandwich. Homework's very fat.

Russell Hoban

Hot Line

Our daughter, Alicia,
Had just turned sixteen,
And was earning the title
Of "Telephone Queen."

For her birthday we gave her
Her own private phone
Along with instructions
To leave ours alone.

Now we still catch her using
Our line, with the stall,
"I can't tie mine up, Mom,
I might get a call."

Louella Dunann

Homework

What is it about homework
That makes me want to write
My Great Aunt Myrt to thank her for
The sweater that's too tight?

What is it about homework
That makes me pick up socks
That stink from days and days of wear,
Then clean the litter box?

What is it about homework
That makes me volunteer
To take the garbage out before
The bugs and flies appear?

What is it about homework
That makes me wash my hair
And take an hour combing out
The snags and tangles there?

What is it about homework?
You know, I wish I knew,
'Cause nights when I've got homework
I've got much too much to do!

Jane Yolen

I'm Alone in the Evening

I'm alone in the evening
when the family sits
reading and sleeping
and I watch the fire in close
to see flame goblins
wriggling out of their caves
for the evening

Later I'm alone
when the bath has gone cold around me
and I have put my foot
beneath the cold tap
where it can dribble
through valleys between my toes
out across the white plain of my foot
and bibble bibble into the sea

I'm alone
when mum's switched out the light
my head against the pillow
listening to ca thump ca thump
in the middle of my ears.
It's my heart.

Michael Rosen

The Winning of the TV West

When twilight comes to Prairie Street
On every TV channel,
The kids watch men with blazing guns
In jeans and checkered flannel.
Partner, the West is wild tonight—
There's going to be a battle
Between the sheriff's posse and
The gang that stole the cattle.
On every screen on Prairie Street
The sheriff roars his order:
"We've got to head those hombres off
Before they reach the border."
Clippity-clop and bangity-bang
The lead flies left and right.
Paradise Valley is freed again
Until tomorrow night.
And all the kids on Prairie Street
Over and under ten
Can safely go to dinner now . . .
The West is won again.

John T. Alexander

The Middle of the Night

This is a song to be sung at night
When nothing is left of you and the light
When the cats don't bark
And the mice don't moo
And the nightmares come and nuzzle you
When there's blackness in the cupboards
And the closet and the hall
And a tipping, tapping, rapping
In the middle of the wall
When the lights have one by one gone out
All over everywhere
And a shadow by the curtains
Bumps a shadow by the chair
Then you hide beneath your pillow
With your eyes shut very tight
And you sing
"There's nothing sweeter than
The middle of the night.
I'm extremely fond of shadows
And I really must confess
That cats and bats don't scare me.
Well, they couldn't scare me less
And most of all I like the things
That slide and slip and creep."
It really is surprising
How fast you fall asleep.

Karla Kuskin

Two People

She reads the paper,
while he turns on TV;
she likes the mountains,
he craves the sea.

He'd rather drive,
she'll take the plane;
he waits for sunshine;
she walks in the rain.

He gulps down cold drinks,
she sips at hot;
he asks, "Why go?"
She asks, "Why not?"

In just about everything
they disagree,
but they love one another
and they both love me.

Eve Merriam

Our House

Our house is small—
The lawn and all
Can scarcely hold the flowers,
Yet every bit,
The whole of it,
Is precious, for it's ours!

From door to door,
From roof to floor,
From wall to wall we love it;
We wouldn't change
For something strange
One shabby corner of it!

The space complete
In cubic feet
From cellar floor to rafter
Just measures right,
And not too tight,
For us, and friends, and laughter!

Dorothy Brown Thompson

I'M HUNGRY!

I'm hungry, so I think I'll take
a bite or two of lunch,
a pizza and a chocolate cake,
some peanut butter crunch,
a healthy slice of apple pie,
a pound or so of ham,
a stack of waffles (two feet high)
with boysenberry jam.

I'll follow with a dozen eggs
(I'll scramble them, I guess)
and six or seven turkey legs
(I could not do with less),
some rhino roast and hippo stew
and fresh fillet of horse,
then rest a minute (maybe two)
and start the second course.

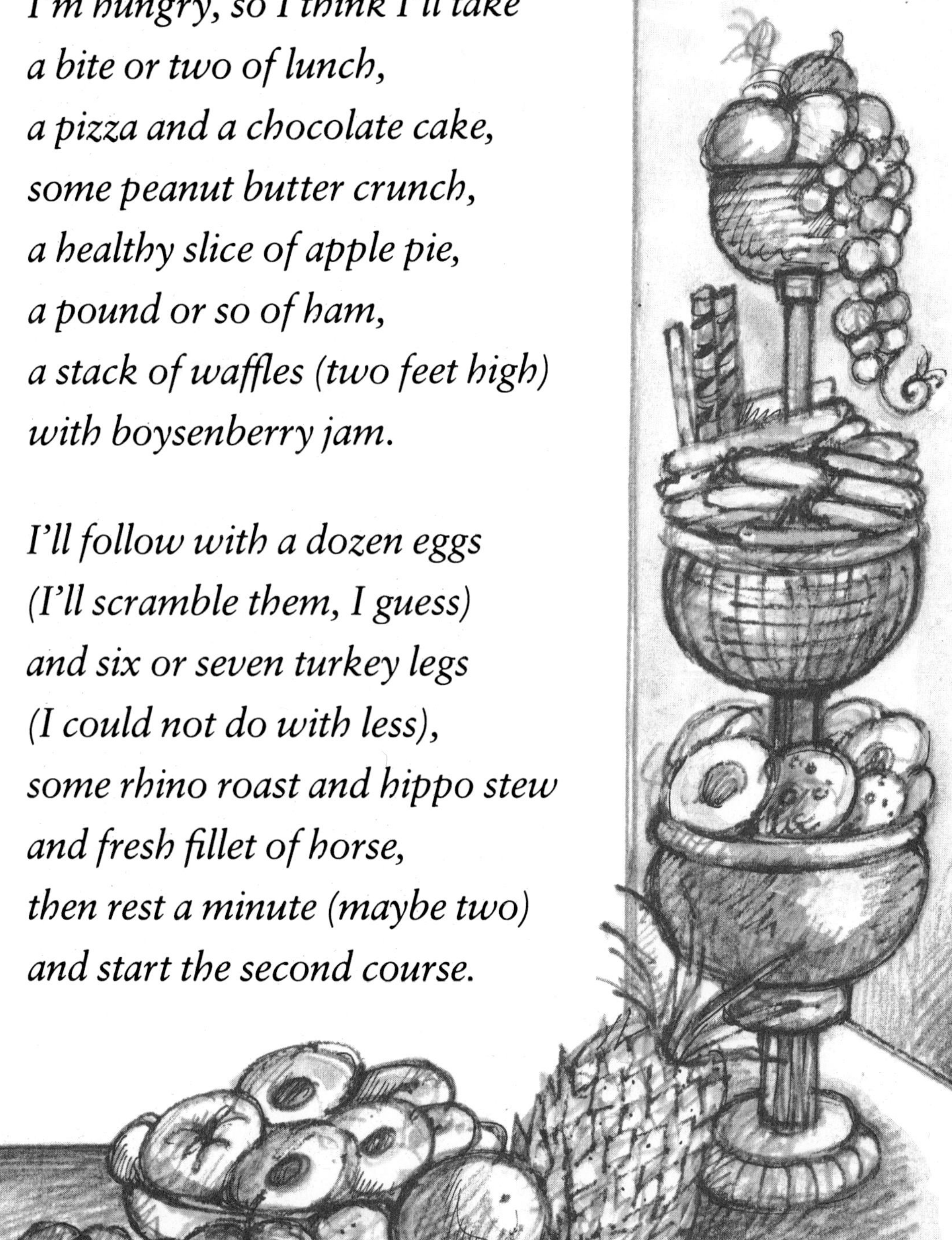

My Mouth

stays shut
      but
food just
finds
    a way

        my tongue says
we are
    full today
    but
      teeth just
        grin
  and
  say
    come in

i am always hungry

Arnold Adoff

Turtle Soup

Beautiful Soup, so rich and green,
Waiting in a hot tureen !
Who for such dainties would not stoop ?
Soup of the evening, beautiful Soup !
Soup of the evening, beautiful Soup !
    Beau—ootiful Soo—oop !
    Beau—ootiful Soo—oop !
Soo—oop of the e—e—evening,
    Beautiful, beautiful Soup !

Beautiful Soup ! Who cares for fish,
Game, or any other dish ?
Who would not give all else for two
pennyworth only of beautiful Soup ?
Pennyworth only of beautiful Soup?
    Beau—ootiful Soo—oop !
    Beau—ootiful Soo—oop !
Soo—oop of the e—e—evening,
    Beautiful, beauti—FUL SOUP !

Lewis Carroll

This Is Just to Say

I have eaten
the plums
that were in
the icebox

and which
you were probably
saving
for breakfast

Forgive me
they were delicious
so sweet
and so cold.

William Carlos Williams

Tomorrow's the Fair

Tomorrow's the fair,
And I shall be there,
Stuffing my guts
With gingerbread nuts.

Anonymous

Egg Thoughts

Soft-Boiled

I do not like the way you slide,
I do not like your soft inside,
I do not like you many ways,
And I could do for many days
Without a soft-boiled egg.

Sunny-Side-Up

With their yolks and whites all runny
They are looking at me funny.

Sunny-Side-Down

Lying face-down on the plate
On their stomachs there they wait.

Poached

Poached eggs on toast, why do you shiver
With such a funny little quiver?

Scrambled

I eat as well as I am able,
But some falls underneath the table.

Hard-Boiled

With so much suffering today
Why do them any other way?

Russell Hoban

Mummy Slept Late and Daddy Fixed Breakfast

Daddy fixed the breakfast.
He made us each a waffle.
It looked like gravel pudding.
It tasted something awful.

"Ha, ha," he said, "I'll try again.
This time I'll get it right."
But what *I* got was in between
Bituminous and anthracite.

"A little too well done? Oh well,
I'll have to start all over."
That time what landed on my plate
Looked like a manhole cover.

I tried to cut it with a fork:
The fork gave off a spark.
I tried a knife and twisted it
Into a question mark.

I tried it with a hack-saw.
I tried it with a torch.
It didn't even make a dent.
It didn't even scorch.

The next time Dad gets breakfast
When Mommy's sleeping late,
I think I'll skip the waffles.
I'd sooner eat the plate!

John Ciardi

Oodles of Noodles

I love noodles. Give me oodles.
Make a mound up to the sun.
Noodles are my favorite foodles.
I eat noodles by the ton.

Lucia and James L. Hymes, Jr.

148

Taste of Purple

Grapes hang purple
In their bunches,
Ready for
September lunches.
Gather them, no
Minutes wasting.
Purple is
Delicious tasting.

Leland B. Jacobs

Meg's Egg

Meg
Likes
A *reg*ular egg
Not a poached
Or a fried
But a *reg*ular egg
Not a deviled
Or coddled
Or scrambled
Or boiled
But an *eggular*
Megular
Regular
Egg!

Mary Ann Hoberman

Pie Problem

If I eat one more piece of pie, I'll die!
If I can't have one more piece of pie, I'll die!
So since it's all decided I must die,
I might as well have one more piece of pie.
MMMM—OOOH—MY!
Chomp—Gulp—'Bye.

Shel Silverstein

Celery

Celery, raw,
Develops the jaw,
But celery, stewed,
Is more quietly chewed.

Ogden Nash

Chocolate Cake

Chocolate cake
chocolate cake
that's the one
I'll help you make
Flour soda
salt are sifted
butter sugar
cocoa lifted
by the eggs
then mix the whole
grease the pans
I'll lick the bowl
Chocolate caked
chocolate caked
that's what I'll be
when it's baked.

Nina Payne

Chocolate Chocolate

i
love
        you so
                i
want
        to
marry
        you
        and
live
        forever
                in the
                flavor
of your
        brown

Arnold Adoff

Patience

Chocolate Easter bunny
    In a jelly bean nest,
I'm saving you for very last
    Because I love you best.
I'll only take a nibble
    From the tip of your ear
And one bite from the other side
    So that you won't look queer.
Yum, you're so delicious!
    I didn't mean to eat
Your chocolate tail till Tuesday.
    Oops! There go your feet!
I wonder how your back tastes
    With all that chocolate hair.
I never thought your tummy
    Was only filled with air!
Chocolate Easter bunny
    In a jelly bean nest,
I'm saving you for very last
    Because I love you best.

Bobbi Katz

Little Bits of Soft-Boiled Egg

Little bits of soft-boiled egg
Spread along the table leg
Annoy a parent even more
Than toast and jam dropped on the floor.
(When you're bashing on the ketchup
Keep in mind where it might fetch up.)
Try to keep the food you eat
Off your clothes and off your seat,
On your plate and fork and knife.
This holds true throughout your life.

Fay Maschler

My Little Sister

My little sister
Likes to eat.
But when she does
She's not too neat.
The trouble is
She doesn't know
Exactly where
The food should go!

William Wise

150

Accidentally

Once—I didn't mean to,
but that
was that—
I yawned in the sunshine
and swallowed a gnat.

I'd rather eat mushrooms
and bullfrogs' legs,
I'd rather have pepper
all over my eggs

than open my mouth
on a sleepy day
and close on a gnat
going down that way.

It tasted sort of salty.
It didn't hurt a bit.
I accidentally ate a gnat
and that
was
it!

Maxine W. Kumin

A Thousand Hairy Savages

A thousand hairy savages
Sitting down to lunch
Gobble gobble glup glup
Munch munch munch.

Spike Milligan

I Eat My Peas with Honey

I eat my peas with honey;
I've done it all my life.
It makes the peas taste funny,
But it keeps them on the knife.

Anonymous

I Raised a Great Hullabaloo

I raised a great hullabaloo
When I found a large mouse in my stew,
  Said the waiter, "Don't shout
  And wave it about,
Or the rest will be wanting one, too!"

Anonymous

The Worm

When the earth is turned in spring
The worms are fat as anything.

And birds come flying all around
To eat the worms right off the ground.

They like worms just as much as I
Like bread and milk and apple pie.

And once, when I was very young,
I put a worm right on my tongue.

I didn't like the taste a bit,
And so I didn't swallow it.

But oh, it makes my Mother squirm
Because she *thinks* I ate that worm!

Ralph Bergengren

Twickham Tweer

Shed a tear for Twickham Tweer
who ate uncommon meals,
who often peeled bananas
and then only ate the peels,
who emptied jars of marmalade
and only ate the jars,
and only ate the wrappers
off of chocolate candy bars.

When Twickham cooked a chicken
he would only eat the bones,
he discarded scoops of ice cream
though he always ate the cones,
he'd boil a small potato
but he'd only eat the skin,
and pass up canned asparagus
to gobble down the tin.

He sometimes dined on apple cores
and bags of peanut shells,
on cottage cheese containers,
cellophane from caramels,
but Twickham Tweer passed on last year,
that odd and novel man,
when he fried an egg one morning
and then ate the frying pan.

Jack Prelutsky

*Soliloquy of a Tortoise
on Revisiting
the Lettuce Beds
After an Interval of One Hour
While Supposed
to Be
Sleeping
in a Clump
of Blue Hollyhocks*

One cannot have enough
of this delicious stuff!

E.V. Rieu

The Pizza

Look at itsy-bitsy Mitzi!
See her figure slim and ritzy!
She eatsa
Pizza!
Greedy Mitzi!
She no longer itsy-bitsy!

Ogden Nash

Mr. Pratt

Mr. Pratt has never left
A single crumb of bread,
Which may explain why Mrs. Pratt
Looks lean and underfed.

I once asked Mr. Pratt to leave
His wife a crumb of bread.
"Do you suggest," he shrieked at me,
"That I be thin instead?"

"I only thought," I answered true,
"That were you not so fat,
There might be room for me to see
A glimpse of Mrs. Pratt."

Myra Cohn Livingston

Sneaky Bill

I'm Sneaky Bill, I'm terrible mean and vicious,
I steal all the cashews
    from the mixed-nuts dishes;
I eat all the icing but I won't touch the cake,
And what you won't give me,
    I'll go ahead and take.

I gobble up the cherries from everyone's drinks,
And whenever there are sausages
    I grab a dozen links;
I take both drumsticks if
    there's turkey or chicken,
And the biggest strawberries
    are what I'm pickin';

I make sure I get the finest chop on the plate,
And I'll eat the portions of anyone who's late!

I'm always on the spot before the dinner bell—
I guess I'm pretty awful,
                    but
                I
                    do
                        eat
                            well!

William Cole

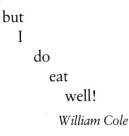

SOME PEOPLE
I KNOW

Some people I know like to chatter,
while others speak hardly a word;
some think there is nothing the matter
with being completely absurd;
some are impossibly serious,
while others are absolute fun;
some are reserved and mysterious,
while others shine bright as the sun.

Some people I know appear sour,
but many seem pleasant and sweet;
some have the grace of a flower,
while others trip over their feet;
some are as still as a steeple,
while some need to fidget and fuss;
yet every last one of these people
is somehow exactly like us.

Routine

No matter what we are and who,
Some duties everyone must do:

A Poet puts aside his wreath
To wash his face and brush his teeth,

And even Earls
Must comb their curls,

And even Kings
Have underthings.

Arthur Guiterman

Some People

Isn't it strange some people make
   You feel so tired inside,
Your thoughts begin to shrivel up
   Like leaves all brown and dried!

But when you're with some other ones,
   It's stranger still to find
Your thoughts as thick as fireflies
   All shiny in your mind!

Rachel Field

People

Some people talk and talk
and never say a thing.
Some people look at you
and birds begin to sing.

Some people laugh and laugh
and yet you want to cry.
Some people touch your hand
and music fills the sky.

Charlotte Zolotow

Daddy Fell into the Pond

Everyone grumbled. The sky was gray.
We had nothing to do and nothing to say.
We were nearing the end of a dismal day,
And there seemed to be nothing beyond,
   THEN
   Daddy fell into the pond!

And everyone's face grew merry and bright,
And Timothy danced for sheer delight.
"Give me the camera, quick, oh quick!
He's crawling out of the duckweed." *Click!*

Then the gardener suddenly slapped his knee,
And doubled up, shaking silently,
And the ducks all quacked as if they were daft
And it sounded as if the old drake laughed.

Oh, there wasn't a thing that didn't respond
   WHEN
   Daddy fell into the pond!

Alfred Noyes

Thoughts on Talkers

Some people talk in a telephone
And some people talk in a hall;
Some people talk in a whisper,
And some people talk in a drawl;
And some people talk-and-talk-and-talk-and-talk-and-talk
And never say anything at all.

Walter R. Brooks

Smart

My dad gave me one dollar bill
'Cause I'm his smartest son,
And I swapped it for two shiny quarters
'Cause two is more than one!

And then I took the quarters
And traded them to Lou
For three dimes—I guess he don't know
That three is more than two!

Just then, along came old blind Bates
And just 'cause he can't see
He gave me four nickels for my three dimes,
And four is more than three!

And I took the nickels to Hiram Coombs
Down at the seed-feed store,
And the fool gave me five pennies for them,
And five is more than four!

And then I went and showed my dad,
And he got red in the cheeks
And closed his eyes and shook his head—
Too proud of me to speak!

Shel Silverstein

One Misty, Moisty Morning

One misty, moisty morning,
    When cloudy was the weather,
I chanced to meet an old man,
    Clothed all in leather.
He began to compliment
    And I began to grin.
How do you do? And how do you do?
    And how do you do again?

Anonymous

My Brother Bert

Pets are the hobby of my brother Bert.
He used to go to school with a mouse in his shirt.

His hobby it grew, as some hobbies will,
And grew and GREW and GREW until—

Oh don't breathe a word, pretend you haven't heard.
A simply appalling thing has occurred—

The very thought makes me iller and iller:
Bert's brought home a gigantic gorilla!

If you think that's really not such a scare,
What if it quarrels with his grizzly bear?

You still think you could keep your head?
What if the lion from under the bed

And the four ostriches that deposit
Their football eggs in his bedroom closet

And the aardvark out of his bottom drawer
All danced out and joined in the roar?

What if the pangolins were to caper
Out of their nests behind the wallpaper?

With the fifty sorts of bats
That hang on his hatstand like old hats,

And out of a shoebox the excitable platypus
Along with the ocelot or jungle-cattypus?

The wombat, the dingo, the gecko, the grampus—
How they would shake the house with their rumpus!

Not to forget the bandicoot
Who would certainly peer from his battered old boot.

Why it could be a dreadful day,
And what, oh what, would the neighbors say!

Ted Hughes

Uncle

Uncle, whose inventive brains
Kept evolving aeroplanes,
Fell from an enormous height
On my garden lawn, last night.
    Flying is a fatal sport,
    Uncle wrecked the tennis-court.

Harry Graham

Manners

I have an uncle I don't like,
    An aunt I cannot bear:
She chucks me underneath the chin,
    He ruffles up my hair.

Another uncle I adore,
    Another aunty, too:
She shakes me kindly by the hand,
    He says, "How do you do?"

Mariana Griswold Van Rensselaer

Grandpapa

Grandpapa fell down a drain;
Couldn't scramble out again.
Now he's floating down the sewer
There's one grandpapa the fewer.

Harry Graham

Growing Old

When I grow old I hope to be
As beautiful as Grandma Lee.
Her hair is soft and fluffy white.
Her eyes are blue and candle bright.
And down her cheeks are cunning piles
Of little ripples when she smiles.

Rose Henderson

Grandpa Dropped His Glasses

Grandpa dropped his glasses once
In a pot of dye,
And when he put them on again
He saw a purple sky.
Purple birds were rising up
From a purple hill,
Men were grinding purple cider
At a purple mill.
Purple Adeline was playing
With a purple doll,
Little purple dragonflies
Were crawling up the wall.
And at the supper table
He got crazy as a loon
From eating purple apple dumplings
With a purple spoon.

Leroy F. Jackson

Miss Norma Jean Pugh,
FIRST GRADE TEACHER

Full of oatmeal
And gluggy with milk
On a morning in springtime
Soft as silk
When legs feel slow
And bumblebees buzz
And your nose tickles from
Dandelion fuzz
And you long to
Break a few
Cobwebs stuck with
Diamond dew
Stretched right out
In front of you—
When all you want
To do is *feel*
Until it's time for
Another meal,
Or sit right down
In the cool
Green grass
And watch the
Caterpillars pass. . . .
Who cares if

Two and two
Are four or five
Or red or blue?
Who cares whether
Six or seven
Come before or after
Ten or eleven?
Who cares if
C-A-T
Spells cat or rat
Or tit or tat
Or ball or bat?
Well, I do
But I didn't
Used to—
Until MISS NORMA JEAN PUGH!
She's terribly old
As people go
Twenty-one-or-five-or-six
Or so
But she makes a person want to
KNOW!

Mary O'Neill

Godmother

There was an old lady
Who had three faces,
One for everyday,
And one for wearing places—
To meetings and parties,
Dull places like that—
A face that looked well
With a grown-up hat.
But she carried in her pocket
The face of an elf,
And she'd clap it on quick
When she felt like herself.
Sitting in the parlor
Of somebody's house,
She'd reach in her pocket
Sly as a mouse . . .
And there in the corner,
Sipping her tea,
Was a laughing elf-woman
Nobody could see!

Phyllis B. Morden

The Little Boy and the Old Man

Said the little boy, "Sometimes I drop my spoon."
Said the little old man, "I do that too."
The little boy whispered, "I wet my pants."
"I do that too," laughed the little old man.
Said the little boy, "I often cry."
The old man nodded, "So do I."
"But worst of all," said the boy, "it seems
Grown-ups don't pay attention to me."
And he felt the warmth of a wrinkled old hand.
"I know what you mean," said the little old man.

Shel Silverstein

Too Many Daves

Did I ever tell you that Mrs. McCave
Had twenty-three sons and she named them all Dave?
Well, she did. And that wasn't a smart thing to do.
You see, when she wants one and calls out, "Yoo-Hoo!
Come into the house, Dave!" she doesn't get *one*.
All twenty-three Daves of hers come on the run!
This makes things quite difficult at the McCaves'
As you can imagine, with so many Daves.
And often she wishes that, when they were born,
She had named one of them Bodkin Van Horn
And one of them Hoos-Foos. And one of them Snimm.
And one of them Hot-Shot. And one Sunny Jim.
And one of them Shadrack. And one of them Blinkey.
And one of them Stuffy. And one of them Stinkey.
Another one Putt-Putt. Another one Moon Face.
Another one Marvin O'Gravel Balloon Face.
And one of them Ziggy. And one Soggy Muff.
One Buffalo Bill. And one Biffalo Buff.
And one of them Sneepy. And one Weepy Weed.
And one Paris Garters. And one Harris Tweed.
And one of them Sir Michael Carmichael Zutt
And one of them Oliver Boliver Butt
And one of them Zanzibar Buck-Buck McFate . . .
But she didn't do it. And now it's too late.

Dr. Seuss

House. For Sale

The doors are locked,
the gray blinds drawn,
new weeds sprung up
in path and lawn.

For "She is dead,"
I heard them say,
the friend I saw
there every day.

She used to wave
from where she sat
in the front room
nursing a cat.

And always smiled
as I passed by
her little house,
and always I

waved back at her,
and then went on
my way to school;
and now she's gone.

And where's her cat?
Does he now roam
all by himself
without a home?

The boards are up,
and I feel glum
because I know
strangers will come.

No more I'll see
my old friend's face,
nor go again
near that sad place.

Leonard Clark

Jittery Jim

There's room in the bus
For the two of us,
But not for Jittery Jim.

He has a train
And a rocket plane,
He has a seal
That can bark and swim,
And a centipede
With wiggly legs,
And an ostrich
Sitting on ostrich eggs,
And crawfish
Floating in oily kegs!

There's room in the bus
For the two of us,
But we'll shut the door on *him*

William Jay Smith

Tombstone

Here lies
A bully
Who wasn't so wise.
He picked on
A fellow
Who was his own size.

Lucia M. and James L. Hymes, Jr.

Air Traveler

He comes from afar
In a silver cigar
And
    walks
        down
            the
                ramp
Like a heavyweight champ.

Lillian Morrison

On a Bad Singer

Swans sing before they die—'twere no bad thing
Should certain persons die before they sing.

Samuel Taylor Coleridge

Doctor Emmanuel

Doctor Emmanuel Harrison-Hyde
Has a very big head with brains inside.
I wonder what happens inside the brains
That Doctor Emmanuel's head contains.

James Reeves

Hog-Calling Competition

A bull-voiced young fellow of Pawling
Competes in the meets for hog-calling;
   The people applaud,
   And the judges are awed,
But the hogs find it simply appalling.

Morris Bishop

Old Quin Queeribus

Old Quin Queeribus—
   He loved his garden so,
He wouldn't have a rake around,
   A shovel or a hoe.

For each potato's eyes he bought
   Fine spectacles of gold,
And mufflers for the corn, to keep
   Its ears from getting cold.

On every head of lettuce green—
   What do you think of that?—
And every head of cabbage, too,
   He tied a garden hat.

Old Quin Queeribus—
   He loved his garden so,
He couldn't eat his growing things,
   He only let them grow!

Nancy Byrd Turner

Jonathan Bing

Poor old Jonathan Bing
Went out in his carriage to visit the King,
But everyone pointed and said, "Look at that!
Jonathan Bing has forgotten his hat!"
(He'd forgotten his hat!)

Poor old Jonathan Bing
Went home and put on a new hat for the King,
But up by the palace a soldier said, "Hi!
You can't see the King; you've forgotten your
    tie!"
(He'd forgotten his tie!)

Poor old Jonathan Bing,
He put on a *beautiful* tie for the King,
But when he arrived an Archbishop said, "Ho!
You can't come to court in pajamas, you know!"

Poor old Jonathan Bing
Went home and addressed a short note to the
    King:

    If you please will excuse me
    I won't come to tea;
    For home's the best place for
    All people like me!

Beatrice Curtis Brown

There Was an Old Man with a Beard

There was an Old Man with a beard,
Who said, "It is just as I feared!—
Two Owls and a Hen, four Larks and a Wren,
Have all built their nests in my beard!"

Edward Lear

Poor Old Lady

Poor old lady, she swallowed a fly.
I don't know why she swallowed a fly.
Poor old lady, I think she'll die.

Poor old lady, she swallowed a spider.
It squirmed and wriggled and turned inside her.
She swallowed the spider to catch the fly.
I don't know why she swallowed a fly.
Poor old lady, I think she'll die.

Poor old lady, she swallowed a bird.
How absurd! She swallowed a bird.
She swallowed the bird to catch the spider,
She swallowed the spider to catch the fly,
I don't know why she swallowed a fly.
Poor old lady, I think she'll die.

Poor old lady, she swallowed a cat.
Think of that! She swallowed a cat.
She swallowed the cat to catch the bird.
She swallowed the bird to catch the spider.
She swallowed the spider to catch the fly,
I don't know why she swallowed a fly.
Poor old lady, I think she'll die.

Poor old lady, she swallowed a dog.
She went the whole hog when she swallowed the dog.
She swallowed the dog to catch the cat,
She swallowed the cat to catch the bird,
She swallowed the bird to catch the spider.
She swallowed the spider to catch the fly,
I don't know why she swallowed a fly.
Poor old lady, I think she'll die.

Poor old lady, she swallowed a cow.
I don't know how she swallowed the cow.
She swallowed the cow to catch the dog,
She swallowed the dog to catch the cat,
She swallowed the cat to catch the bird,
She swallowed the bird to catch the spider,
She swallowed the spider to catch the fly,
I don't know why she swallowed a fly.
Poor old lady, I think she'll die.

Poor old lady, she swallowed a horse.
She died, of course.

Anonymous

Fatty, Fatty, Boom-a-latty

Fatty, Fatty, Boom-a-latty;
    This is the way he goes!
He is so large around the waist,
    He cannot see his toes!

This is Mr. Skinny Linny;
    See his long lean face!
Instead of a regular suit of clothes,
    He wears an umbrella case!

Anonymous

Solomon Grundy

Solomon Grundy,
Born on a Monday,
Christened on Tuesday,
Married on Wednesday,
Took ill on Thursday,
Worse on Friday,
Died on Saturday,
Buried on Sunday,
This is the end
Of Solomon Grundy.

Anonymous

Mr. Kartoffel

Mr. Kartoffel's a whimsical man;
He drinks his beer from a watering-can,
And for no good reason that I can see
He fills his pockets with china tea.
He parts his hair with a knife and fork
And takes his ducks for a Sunday walk.
Says he, "If my wife and I should choose
To wear our stockings outside our shoes,
Plant tulip-bulbs in the baby's pram
And eat tobacco instead of jam,
And fill the bath with cauliflowers,
That's nobody's business at all but ours."

Says Mrs. K., "I may choose to travel
With a sack of grass or a sack of gravel,
Or paint my toes, one black, one white,
Or sit on a birds' nest half the night—
But whatever I do that is rum or rare,
I rather think that it's my affair.
So fill up your pockets with stamps and string,
And let us be ready for anything!"
Says Mr. K. to his whimsical wife,
"How can we face the storms of life,
Unless we are ready for anything?
So if you've provided the stamps and string,
Let us pump up the saddle and harness the horse
And fill him with carrots and custard and sauce,
Let us leap on him lightly and give him a shove
And it's over the sea and away, my love!"

James Reeves

Aunt Sponge and Aunt Spiker

"I look and smell," Aunt Sponge declared, "as
    lovely as a rose!
Just feast your eyes upon my face, observe my
    shapely nose!
Behold my heavenly silky locks!
And if I take off both my socks
You'll see my dainty toes."
"But don't forget," Aunt Spiker cried, "how much
    your tummy shows!"

Aunt Sponge went red. Aunt Spiker said, "My
    sweet, you cannot win,
Behold MY gorgeous curvy shape, my teeth, my
    charming grin!
Oh, beauteous me! How I adore
My radiant looks! And please ignore
The pimple on my chin."
"My dear old trout!" Aunt Sponge cried out. "You're
    only bones and skin!

"Such loveliness as I possess can only truly shine
In Hollywood!" Aunt Sponge declared. "Oh,
    wouldn't that be fine!
I'd capture all the nations' hearts!
They'd give me all the leading parts!
The stars would all resign!"
"I think you'd make," Aunt Spiker said, "a lovely
    Frankenstein."

Roald Dahl

The Sugar Lady

There is an old lady who lives down the hall,
Wrinkled and gray and toothless and small.
At seven already she's up,
Going from door to door with a cup.
"Do you have any sugar?" she asks,
Although she's got more than you.
"Do you have any sugar," she asks,
Hoping you'll talk for a minute or two.

Frank Asch

Lord Cray

The sight of his guests filled Lord Cray
At breakfast with horrid dismay,
  So he launched off the spoons
  The pits from his prunes
At their heads as they neared the buffet.

Edward Gorey

Together

Because we do
All things together
All things improve,
Even weather.

Our daily meat
And bread taste better,
Trees are greener,
Rain is wetter.

Paul Engle

The Opposite of Two

What is the opposite of *two*?
A lonely me, a lonely you.

Richard Wilbur

Sir Smasham Uppe

Good afternoon, Sir Smasham Uppe!
We're having tea: do take a cup.
Sugar and milk? Now let me see—
Two lumps, I think? . . . Good gracious me!
The silly thing slipped off your knee!
Pray don't apologize, old chap:
A very trivial mishap!
So clumsy of you? How absurd!
My dear Sir Smasham, not a word!
Now do sit down and have another,
And tell us all about your brother—
You know, the one who broke his head.
Is the poor fellow still in bed?—
A chair—allow me, sir! . . . Great Scott!
That *was* a nasty smash! Eh, what?
Oh, not at all: the chair was old—
Queen Anne, or so we have been told.
We've got at least a dozen more:
Just leave the pieces on the floor.
I want you to admire our view:
Come nearer to the window, do;
And look how beautiful . . . Tut, tut!
You didn't see that it was shut?
I hope you are not badly cut!
Not hurt? A fortunate escape!
Amazing! Not a single scrape!
And now, if you have finished tea,
I fancy you might like to see
A little thing or two I've got.
That china plate? Yes, worth a lot:
A beauty too . . . Ah, there it goes!
I trust it didn't hurt your toes?
Your elbow brushed it off the shelf?
Of course: I've done the same myself.
And now, my dear Sir Smasham—Oh,
You surely don't intend to go?
You *must* be off? Well, come again.
So glad you're fond of porcelain!

E.V. Rieu

NONSENSE !

Nonsense? That's what makes no sense;
a walrus waltzing on a fence,
cats in vats of cheese and chowder,
weasels sniffing sneezing powder,
elephants with bright umbrellas
dancing sprightly tarantellas,
tigers dressed in spotted sweaters
playing chess and writing letters.

Nonsense? Lizards clanging cymbals,
flying eggs and weeping thimbles,
sleeping prunes and crooning poodles,
hopping spoons and creeping noodles,
schools of fish that moo like cattle,
bloomers marching into battle,
pigs with wigs and purple wings.
Nonsense! All these silly things.

Toot! Toot!

A peanut sat on a railroad track,
His heart was all a-flutter;
The five-fifteen came rushing by—
Toot! toot! peanut butter!

Anonymous

Jabberwocky

'Twas brillig, and the slithy toves
    Did gyre and gimble in the wabe:
All mimsy were the borogoves,
    And the mome raths outgrabe.

"Beware the Jabberwock, my son!
    The jaws that bite, the claws that catch!
Beware the Jubjub bird, and shun
    The frumious Bandersnatch!"

He took his vorpal sword in hand:
    Long time the manxome foe he sought—
So rested he by the Tumtum tree,
    And stood awhile in thought.

And, as in uffish thought he stood,
    The Jabberwock, with eyes of flame,
Came whiffling through the tulgey wood,
    And burbled as it came!

One, two! One, two! And through and through
    The vorpal blade went snicker-snack!
He left it dead, and with its head
    He went galumphing back.

"And hast thou slain the Jabberwock?
    Come to my arms, my beamish boy!
O frabjous day! Callooh! Callay!"
    He chortled in his joy.

'Twas brillig, and the slithy toves
    Did gyre and gimble in the wabe:
All mimsy were the borogoves,
    And the mome raths outgrabe.

Lewis Carroll

Higglety, Pigglety, Pop!

Higglety, pigglety, pop!
The dog has eaten the mop;
    The pig's in a hurry,
    The cat's in a flurry,
Higglety, pigglety, pop!

Samuel Goodrich

The Lobsters and the Fiddler Crab

The lobsters came ashore one night
  In the merry month of June,
And coaxed the fiddler crab to play
  A rollicking tango tune.

The lobsters danced, the fiddler played
  Till morning, rosy red,
Chased the dancers into the sea
  And the fiddler home to bed!

Frederick J. Forster

McIntosh Apple

McIntosh apple
Has nice rosy cheeks
Romaine lettuce
Turns green when she speaks
Cherry tomato
Has gorgeous red hair
But I'm mashed potatoes
And fall down the stairs.

Steven Kroll

The Common Cormorant

The common cormorant or shag
Lays eggs inside a paper bag
The reason you will see no doubt
It is to keep the lightning out.
But what these unobservant birds
Have never noticed is that herds
Of wandering bears may come with buns
And steal the bags to hold the crumbs.

Christopher Isherwood

On the Ning Nang Nong

On the Ning Nang Nong
Where the Cows go Bong!
And the Monkeys all say Boo!
There's a Nong Nang Ning
Where the trees go Ping!
And the tea pots Jibber Jabber Joo.
On the Nong Ning Nang
All the mice go Clang!
And you just can't catch 'em when they do!
So it's Ning Nang Nong!
Cows go Bong!
Nong Nang Ning!
Trees go Ping!
Nong Ning Nang!
The mice go Clang!
What a noisy place to belong,
Is the Ning Nang Ning Nang Nong! !

Spike Milligan

The Butterfly's Ball

Come take up your hats, and away let us haste,
To the Butterfly's Ball, and the Grasshopper's Feast.
The trumpeter Gadfly has summoned the crew,
And the revels are now only waiting for you.

On the smooth-shaven grass by the side of a wood,
Beneath a broad oak which for ages has stood,
See the children of earth and the tenants of air,
For an evening's amusement together repair.

And there came the Beetle, so blind and so black,
Who carried the Emmet, his friend, on his back.
And there came the Gnat, and the Dragonfly too,
And all their relations, green, orange, and blue.

And there came the Moth, with her plumage of down,
And the Hornet, with jacket of yellow and brown;
Who with him the Wasp, his companion, did bring,
But they promised that evening, to lay by their sting.

Then the sly little Dormouse crept out of his hole,
And led to the feast his blind cousin the Mole.
And the Snail, with his horns peeping out of his shell,
Came, fatigued with the distance, the length of an ell.

A mushroom their table, and on it was laid
A water-dock leaf, which a tablecloth made.
The viands were various, to each of their taste,
And the Bee brought the honey to sweeten the feast.

With steps most majestic the Snail did advance,
And he promised the gazers a minuet to dance;
But they all laughed so loud that he drew in his head,
And went in his own little chamber to bed.

Then, as evening gave way to the shadows of night,
Their watchman, the Glow-worm, came out with his light.
So home let us hasten, while yet we can see;
For no watchman is waiting for you and for me.

William Roscoe

Way Down South

Way down South where bananas grow,
A grasshopper stepped on an elephant's toe.
The elephant said, with tears in his eyes,
"Pick on somebody your own size."

Anonymous

The Contrary Waiter

A tarsier worked as a waiter.
He wore a stiff collar and tie.
He said, "Of all creatures who cater,
None are calm and undaunted as I."

When asked to serve mutton with mustard,
He'd scribble a note on a pad
And return with a half-eaten custard
And say it was all that they had.

When a cup of hot cocoa was ordered,
His eyes would defiantly gleam;
He'd bring back asparagus bordered
With heaps of vanilla ice cream.

If cucumber salad was wanted,
The customer suffered a shock:
The tarsier, calm and undaunted,
Brought rice pudding, stuffed in a sock.

He never brought what was requested.
There was always a terrible risk.
And customers—if they protested—
Were splattered with hot oyster bisque.

One day an immense alligator
Sat down at a table to sup.
He grapped the contemptible waiter
And ate him contemptibly up.

Edgar Parker

Whoops!

A horse and a flea and three blind mice
Sat on a curbstone shooting dice.
The horse he slipped and fell on the flea.
The flea said, "Whoops, there's a horse on me."

Anonymous

The Duel

The gingham dog and the calico cat
    Side by side on the table sat;
    'Twas half-past twelve, and (what do you think!)
Nor one nor t'other had slept a wink!
    The old Dutch clock and the Chinese plate
    Appeared to know as sure as fate
There was going to be a terrible spat.
    (I wasn't there; I simply state
    What was told to me by the Chinese plate!)

The gingham dog went "bow-wow-wow!"
And the calico cat replied "mee-ow!"
The air was littered, an hour or so,
With bits of gingham and calico,
    While the old Dutch clock in the chimney-place
    Up with its hands before its face,
For it always dreaded a family row!
    (Now mind: I'm only telling you
    What the old Dutch clock declares is true!)

The Chinese plate looked very blue,
And wailed, "Oh dear! what shall we do!"
But the gingham dog and the calico cat
Wallowed this way and tumbled that,
Employing every tooth and claw
In the awfullest way you ever saw—
And, oh! how the gingham and calico flew!
    (Don't fancy I exaggerate—
    I got my news from the Chinese plate!)

Next morning, where the two had sat
They found no trace of dog or cat;
And some folks think unto this day
That burglars stole that pair away!
    But the truth about the cat and pup
    Is this: they ate each other up!
Now what do you really think of that!
    (The old Dutch clock it told me so,
    And that is how I came to know.)

Eugene Field

The Owl and the Pussy-Cat

I

The Owl and the Pussy-cat went to sea
   In a beautiful pea-green boat,
They took some honey, and plenty of money,
   Wrapped up in a five-pound note.
The Owl looked up to the stars above,
   And sang to a small guitar,
"O lovely Pussy! O Pussy, my love,
     What a beautiful Pussy you are,
       You are,
       You are!
What a beautiful Pussy you are!"

II

Pussy said to the Owl, "You elegant fowl!
   How charmingly sweet you sing!
O let us be married! too long we have tarried:
   But what shall we do for a ring?"
They sailed away, for a year and a day,
   To the land where the Bong-tree grows
And there in a wood a Piggy-wig stood
   With a ring at the end of his nose,
       His nose,
       His nose,
   With a ring at the end of his nose.

III

"Dear Pig, are you willing to sell for one shilling
   Your ring?" Said the Piggy, "I will."
So they took it away, and were married next day
   By the Turkey who lives on the hill.
They dined on mince, and slices of quince,
   Which they ate with a runcible spoon;
And hand in hand, on the edge of the sand,
   They danced by the light of the moon,
       The moon,
       The moon,
They danced by the light of the moon.

Edward Lear

The Hare and the Pig

When the hare and the pig had some pleasure to plan,
They each found they had much better fun
If they planned it together and both of them said,
"Surely two heads are better than one!"

But the hare had the toothache, the pig got the mumps,
Then they cried, "Oh, just one head will do!
Just to think what we'd suffer if each had two heads!
Surely one head is better than two!"

L. J. Bridgman

The Alligator

The alligator chased his tail
Which hit him on the snout;
He nibbled, gobbled, swallowed it,
And turned right inside-out.

Mary Macdonald

The Lizard

The Time to Tickle a Lizard,
Is Before, or Right After, a Blizzard.
Now the place to begin
Is just under his Chin—
And here's more Advice:
Don't Poke more than Twice
At an Intimate Place like his Gizzard.

Theodore Roethke

The Serpent

There was a Serpent who had to sing.
There was. There was.
He simply gave up Serpenting.
Because. Because.

He didn't like his Kind of Life;
He couldn't find a proper Wife;
He was a Serpent with a soul;
He got no Pleasure down his Hole.
And so, of course, he had to Sing,
And Sing he did, like Anything!
The Birds, they were, they were Astounded;
And various Measures Propounded
To stop the Serpent's Awful Racket:
They bought a Drum. He wouldn't Whack it.
They sent—you always send—to Cuba
And got a Most Commodious Tuba;
They got a Horn, they got a Flute,
But Nothing would suit.
He said, "Look, Birds, all this is futile:
I do *not* like to Bang or Tootle."
And then he cut loose with a Horrible Note
That practically split the Top of his Throat.
"You see," he said, with a Serpent's Leer,
"I'm Serious about my Singing Career!"
And the Woods Resounded with many a Shriek
As the Birds flew off to the End of Next Week.

Theodore Roethke

Had a Little Pig

had a little pig,
fed him in a trough,
Ie got so fat
Iis tail dropped off.
o I got me a hammer,
.nd I got me a nail,
.nd I made my little pig
  brand-new tail.

Anonymous

The Shark

)h, what a lark to fish for shark
    With Grandpapa for bait!
he Shark would be in time for tea
    And Grandpapa be *late*.

J. J. Bell

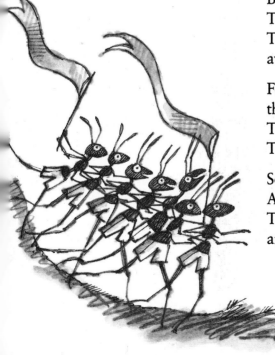

The Ants at the Olympics

At last year's Jungle Olympics,
the Ants were completely outclassed.
In fact, from an entry of sixty-two teams,
the Ants came their usual last.

They didn't win one single medal.
Not that that's a surprise.
The reason was not lack of trying,
but more their unfortunate size.

While the cheetahs won most of the sprinting
and the hippos won putting the shot,
the Ants tried sprinting but couldn't,
and tried to put but could not.

It was sad for the ants 'cause they're sloggers.
They turn out for every event.
With their shorts and their bright orange tee-shirts,
their athletes are proud they are sent.

They came last at the high jump and hurdles,
which they say they'd have won, but they fell.
They came last in the four hundred meters
and last in the swimming as well.

They came last in the long-distance running,
though they say they might have come first.
And they might if the other sixty-one teams
hadn't put in a finishing burst.

But each year they turn up regardless.
They're popular in the parade.
The other teams whistle and cheer them,
aware of the journey they've made.

For the Jungle Olympics in August,
they have to set off New Year's Day.
They didn't arrive the year before last.
They set off but went the wrong way.

So long as they try there's a reason.
After all, it's only a sport.
They'll be back next year to bring up the rear,
and that's an encouraging thought.

Richard Digance

I Asked My Mother

I asked my mother for fifty cents
To see the elephant jump the fence.
He jumped so high that he touched the sky
And never came back till the Fourth of July.

Anonymous

The Animal Fair

I went to the animal fair,
The birds and beasts were there.
The big baboon, by the light of the moon,
Was combing his auburn hair.
The monkey, he got drunk,
And sat on the elephant's trunk.
The elephant sneezed and fell on his knees,
And what became of the monk, the monk?

Anonymous

The Walrus

The Walrus lives on icy floes
And unsuspecting Eskimoes.

Don't bring your wife to Arctic Tundr
A Walrus may bob up from undra.

Michael Flanders

The Purple Cow

I never saw a Purple Cow,
   I never hope to see one;
But I can tell you, anyhow,
   I'd rather see than be one.

Gelett Burgess

Algy Met a Bear

Algy met a bear,
A bear met Algy.
The bear was bulgy,
The bulge was Algy.

Anonymous

Adventures of Isabel

Isabel met an enormous bear,
Isabel, Isabel, didn't care;
The bear was hungry, the bear was ravenous,
The bear's big mouth was cruel and cavernous.
The bear said, Isabel, glad to meet you,
How do, Isabel, now I'll eat you!
Isabel, Isabel, didn't worry,
Isabel didn't scream or scurry.
She washed her hands and she straightened her hair up,
Then Isabel quietly ate the bear up.

Once in a night as black as pitch
Isabel met a wicked old witch.
The witch's face was cross and wrinkled,
The witch's gums with teeth were sprinkled.
Ho ho, Isabel! the old witch crowed,
I'll turn you into an ugly toad!
Isabel, Isabel, didn't worry,
Isabel didn't scream or scurry,
She showed no rage and she showed no rancor,
But she turned the witch into milk and drank her.

Isabel met a hideous giant,
Isabel continued self-reliant.
The giant was hairy, the giant was horrid,
He had one eye in the middle of his forehead.
Good morning, Isabel, the giant said,
I'll grind your bones to make my bread.
Isabel, Isabel, didn't worry,
Isabel didn't scream or scurry.
She nibbled the Zwieback that she always fed off,
And when it was gone, she cut the giant's head off.

Isabel met a troublesome doctor,
He punched and he poked till he really shocked her.
The doctor's talk was of coughs and chills
And the doctor's satchel bulged with pills.
The doctor said unto Isabel,
Swallow this, it will make you well.
Isabel, Isabel, didn't worry,
Isabel didn't scream or scurry.
She took those pills from the pill concocter,
And Isabel calmly cured the doctor.

Ogden Nash

Alligator Pie

Alligator pie, alligator pie,
If I don't get some I think I'm gonna die.
Give away the green grass, give away the sky,
But don't give away my alligator pie.

Alligator stew, alligator stew,
If I don't get some I don't know what I'll do.
Give away my furry hat, give away my shoe,
But don't give away my alligator stew.

Alligator soup, alligator soup,
If I don't get some I think I'm gonna droop.
Give away my hockey-stick, give away my hoop,
But don't give away my alligator soup.

Dennis Lee

Did You Ever Go Fishing?

Did you ever go fishing on a bright sunny day—
Sit on a fence and have the fence give way?
Slide off the fence and rip your pants,
And see the little fishes do the hootchy-kootchy danc

Anonymous

Beela by the Sea

Catch a floater, catch an eel,
Catch a lazy whale,
Catch an oyster by the heel
And put him in a pail.

There's lots of work for Uncle Ike,
Fatty Ford and me
All day long and half the night
At Beela by the sea.

Leroy F. Jackson

You Must Never Bath in an Irish Stew

You must never bath in an Irish Stew
It's a most illogical thing to do
      But should you persist against my reasoning
      Don't fail to add the appropriate seasoning.

Spike Milligan

The Folk Who Live in Backward Town

The folk who live in Backward Town
Are inside out and upside down.
They wear their hats inside their heads
And go to sleep beneath their beds.
They only eat the apple peeling
And take their walks across the ceiling.

Mary Ann Hoberman

Sensitive, Seldom and Sad

Sensitive, Seldom and Sad are we,
As we wend our way to the sneezing sea,
With our hampers full of thistles and fronds
To plant round the edge of the dab-fish ponds;
Oh, so Sensitive, Seldom and Sad—
Oh, so Seldom and Sad.

In the shambling shades of the shelving shore,
We will sing us a song of the Long Before,
And light a red fire and warm our paws
For it's chilly, it is, on the Desolate shores,
For those who are Sensitive, Seldom and Sad,
For those who are Seldom and Sad.

Sensitive, Seldom and Sad we are,
As we wander along through Lands Afar,
To the sneezing sea, where the sea-weeds be,
And the dab-fish ponds that are waiting for we
Who are, Oh, so Sensitive, Seldom and Sad,
Oh, so Seldom and Sad.

Mervyn Peake

Josephine

Josephine, Josephine,
The meanest girl I've ever seen.
Her eyes are red, her hair is green
And she takes baths in gasoline.

Alexander Resnikoff

Father William

"You are old, Father William," the young man said,
    "And your hair has become very white;
And yet you incessantly stand on your head—
    Do you think, at your age, it is right?"

"In my youth," Father William replied to his son,
    "I feared it might injure the brain;
But, now that I'm perfectly sure I have none,
    Why, I do it again and again."

"You are old," said the youth, "as I mentioned before,
    And have grown most uncommonly fat;
Yet you turned a back-somersault in at the door—
    Pray, what is the reason of that?"

"In my youth," said the sage, as he shook his gray locks,
    "I kept all my limbs very supple
By the use of this ointment—one shilling the box—
    Allow me to sell you a couple?"

"You are old," said the youth, "and your jaws are too weak
    For anything tougher than suet;
Yet you finished the goose, with the bones and the beak—
    Pray, how did you manage to do it?"

"In my youth," said his father, "I took to the law,
    And argued each case with my wife;
And the muscular strength which it gave to my jaw
    Has lasted the rest of my life."

"You are old," said the youth, "one would hardly suppose
    That your eye was as steady as ever;
Yet you balanced an eel on the end of your nose—
    What made you so awfully clever?"

"I have answered three questions, and that is enough,"
    Said his father; "don't give yourself airs!
Do you think I can listen all day to such stuff?
    Be off, or I'll kick you downstairs!"

Lewis Carroll

The Twins

In form and feature, face and limb,
    I grew so like my brother,
That folks got taking me for him,
    And each for one another.
It puzzled all our kith and kin,
    It reached an awful pitch;
For one of us was born a twin,
    Yet not a soul knew which.

One day (to make the matter worse),
    Before our names were fixed,
As we were being washed by nurse
    We got completely mixed;
And thus, you see, by Fate's decree
    (Or rather nurse's whim),
My brother John got christened *me*,
    And I got christened *him*.

This fatal likeness even dogged
    My footsteps when at school,
And I was always getting flogged
    For John turned out a fool.
I put this question hopelessly
    To everyone I knew—
What *would* you do, if you were me,
    To prove that you were *you*?

Our close resemblance turned the tide
    Of my domestic life;
For somehow my intended bride
    Became my brother's wife.
In short, year after year the same
    Absurd mistake went on;
And when I died—the neighbors came
    And buried brother John!

Henry S. Leigh

Johnnie Crack and Flossie Snail

Johnnie Crack and Flossie Snail
Kept their baby in a milking pail
Flossie Snail and Johnnie Crack
One would pull it out and one would put it back

O it's my turn now said Flossie Snail
To take the baby from the milking pail
And it's my turn now said Johnnie Crack
To smack it on the head and put it back

Johnny Crack and Flossie Snail
Kept their baby in a milking pail
One would put it back and one would pull it out
And all it had to drink was ale and stout
For Johnnie Crack and Flossie Snail
Always used to say that stout and ale
Was *good* for a baby in a milking pail.

Dylan Thomas

The Snail's Dream

A snail, who had a way, it seems,
Of dreaming very curious dreams,
Once dreamed he was—you'll never guess !—
The Lightning Limited Express !

Oliver Herford

The New Vestments

There lived an old man in the Kingdom of Tess,
Who invented a purely original dress;
And when it was perfectly made and complete,
He opened the door, and walked into the street.

By way of a hat, he'd a loaf of Brown Bread,
In the middle of which he inserted his head;
His Shirt was made up of no end of dead Mice,
The warmth of whose skins was quite fluffy and nice;
His Drawers were of Rabbit-skins; so were his Shoes;
His Stockings were skins—but it is not known whose;
His Waistcoat and Trousers were made of Pork Chops;
His Buttons were Jujubes, and Chocolate Drops;
His Coat was all Pancakes with Jam for a border,
And a girdle of Biscuits to keep it in order;
And he wore over all, as a screen from bad weather,
A Cloak of green Cabbage-leaves stitched all together.

He had walked a short way, when he heard a great noise,
Of all sorts of Beasticles, Birdlings, and Boys;
And from every long street and dark lane in the town
Beasts, Birdles, and Boys in a tumult rushed down.
Two Cows and a half ate his Cabbage-leaf Cloak;
Four Apes seized his Girdle, which vanished like smoke;

Three Kids ate up half of his Pancaky Coat,
And the tails were devoured by an ancient He Goat;
An army of Dogs in a twinkling tore up his
Pork Waistcoat and Trousers to give to their Puppies;
And while they were growling, and mumbling the Chops,
Ten Boys prigged the Jujubes and Chocolate Drops.
He tried to run back to his house, but in vain,
For Scores of fat Pigs came again and again;
They rushed out of stables and hovels and doors,
They tore off his stockings, his shoes, and his drawers;
And now from the housetops with screechings descend,
Striped, spotted, white, black, and gray Cats without end,
They jumped on his shoulders and knocked off his hat,
When Crows, Ducks, and Hens made a mincemeat of that,
They speedily flew at his sleeves in a trice,
And utterly tore up his Shirt of dead Mice;
They swallowed the last of his Shirt with a squall,
Whereon he ran home with no clothes on at all.

And he said to himself as he bolted the door,
"I will not wear a similar dress anymore,
"Anymore, anymore, anymore, nevermore!"

Edward Lear

Pumberly Pott's Unpredictable Niece

Pumberly Pott's unpredictable niece
declared with her usual zeal
that she would devour, by piece after piece,
her uncle's new automobile.

She set to her task very early one morn
by consuming the whole carburetor;
then she swallowed the windshield, the headlights and horn
and the steering wheel just a bit later.

She chomped on the doors, on the handles and locks,
on the valves and the pistons and rings;
on the air pump and fuel pump and spark plugs and shocks
on the brakes and the axles and springs.

When her uncle arrived she was chewing a hash
made of leftover hoses and wires
(she'd just finished eating the clutch and the dash
and the steel-belted radial tires).

"Oh, what have you done to my auto," he cried,
"you strange unpredictable lass?"
"The thing wouldn't work, Uncle Pott," she replied,
and he wept, "It was just out of gas."

Jack Prelutsky

Don't Worry if Your Job Is Small

Don't worry if your job is small,
And your rewards are few.
Remember that the mighty oak,
Was once a nut like you.

Anonymous

Tender-heartedness

Billy, in one of his nice new sashes,
Fell in the fire and was burned to ashes;
Now, although the room grows chilly,
I haven't the heart to poke poor Billy.

Harry Graham

Number Nine, Penwiper Mews

From Number Nine, Penwiper Mews,
There is really abominable news:
    They've discovered a head
    In the box for the bread,
But nobody seems to know whose.

Edward Gorey

A Young Lady of Lynn

There was a young lady of Lynn,
Who was so uncommonly thin
   That when she essayed
   To drink lemonade,
She slipped through the straw and fell in.

Anonymous

Jimmy Jet and His TV Set

I'll tell you the story of Jimmy Jet—
And you know what I tell you is true.
He loved to watch his TV set
Almost as much as you.

He watched all day, he watched all night
Till he grew pale and lean,
From "The Early Show" to "The Late Late Show"
And all the shows between.

He watched till his eyes were frozen wide,
And his bottom grew into his chair.
And his chin turned into a tuning dial,
And antennae grew out of his hair.

And his brains turned into TV tubes,
And his face to a TV screen.
And two knobs saying "VERT." and "HORIZ."
Grew where his ears had been.

And he grew a plug that looked like a tail
So we plugged in little Jim.
And now instead of him watching TV
We all sit around and watch him.

Shel Silverstein

Herbert Glerbett

Herbert Glerbett, rather round,
swallowed sherbet by the pound,
fifty pounds of lemon sherbet
went inside of Herbert Glerbett.

With that glob inside his lap
Herbert Glerbett took a nap,
and as he slept, the boy dissolved,
and from the mess a thing evolved—

a thing that is a ghastly green,
a thing the world had never seen,
a puddle thing, a gooey pile
of something strange that does not smile.

Now if you're wise, and if you're sly,
you'll swiftly pass this creature by,
it is no longer Herbert Glerbett.
Whatever it is, do not disturb it.

Jack Prelutsky

ALPHABET STEW

Words can be stuffy, as sticky as glue,
but words can be tutored to tickle you too,
to rumble and tumble and tingle and sing,
to buzz like a bumblebee, coil like a spring.

Juggle their letters and jumble their sounds,
swirl them in circles and stack them in mounds,
twist them and tease them and turn them about,
teach them to dance upside down, inside out.

Make mighty words whisper and tiny words roar
in ways no one ever had thought of before;
cook an improbable alphabet stew,
and words will reveal little secrets to you.

The Tutor

A tutor who tootled the flute
    Was teaching two tooters to too[t]
Said the two to the tutor,
    "Is it harder to toot,
Or to tutor two tooters to toot?"

Carolyn Wells

A Fly and a Flea in a Flue

A fly and a flea in a flue
Were imprisoned, so what could they do?
    Said the fly, "Let us flee!"
    "Let us fly!" said the flea,
And they flew through a flaw in the flue.

Anonymous

Weather

Whether the weather be fine
Or whether the weather be not,
Whether the weather be cold
Or whether the weather be hot,
We'll weather the weather
Whatever the weather,
Whether we like it or not.

Anonymous

Two Witches

There was a witch
The witch had an itch
The itch was so itchy it
Gave her a twitch.

Another witch
Admired the twitch
So she started twitching
Though she had no itch.

Now both of them twitch
So it's hard to tell which
Witch has the itch and
Which witch has the twitch.

Alexander Resnikoff

The Cow

The cow mainly moos as she chooses to moo
and she chooses to moo as she chooses.

She furthermore chews as she chooses to chew
and she chooses to chew as she muses.

If she chooses to moo she may moo to amuse
or may moo just to moo as she chooses.

If she chooses to chew she may moo as she chews
or may chew just to chew as she muses.

Jack Prelutsky

The Bluffalo

Oh, do not tease the Bluffalo
With quick-step or with shuffalo
When you are in a scuffalo
In Bluffalo's backyard.

For it has quite enoughalo
Of people playing toughalo
And when it gives a cuffalo
It gives it very hard.

But if by chance a scuffalo
Occurs twixt you and Bluffalo,
Pray tempt it with a truffalo
And catch it off its guard.

And while it eats that stuffalo
You can escape the Bluffalo
And with a huff and puffalo
Depart from its backyard.

Jane Yolen

Habits of the Hippopotamus

The hippopotamus is strong
    And huge of head and broad of bustle;
The limbs on which he rolls along
    Are big with hippopotomuscle.

He does not greatly care for sweets
    Like ice cream, apple pie, or custard,
But takes to flavor what he eats
    A little hippopotomustard.

The hippopotamus is true
    To all his principles, and just;
He always tries his best to do
    The things one hippopotomust.

He never rides in trucks or trams,
    In taxicabs or omnibuses,
And so keeps out of traffic jams
    And other hippopotomusses.

Arthur Guiterman

Moses

Moses supposes his toeses are roses,
But Moses supposes erroneously;
For nobody's toeses are posies of roses
As Moses supposes his toeses to be.

Anonymous

Antonio

Antonio, Antonio,
Was tired of living alonio.
    He thought he would woo
    Miss Lissamy Lou,
Miss Lissamy Lucy Molonio.

Antonio, Antonio,
Rode off on his polo-ponio.
    He found the fair maid
    In a bowery shade,
A-sitting and knitting alonio.

Antonio, Antonio,
Said, "If you will be my ownio
    I'll love you true,
    And I'll buy for you,
An icery creamery conio!"

"Oh, nonio, Antonio!
You're far too bleak and bonio!
    And all that I wish,
    You singular fish,
Is that you will quickly begonio."

Antonio, Antonio,
He uttered a dismal moanio;
    Then ran off and hid
    (Or I'm told that he did)
In the Antarctical Zonio.

Laura E. Richards

Mr. Bidery's Spidery Garden

Poor old Mr. Bidery.
His garden's awfully spidery:
Bugs use it as a hidery.

In April it was seedery,
By May a mass of weedery;
And oh, the bugs! How greedery.

White flowers out or buddery,
Potatoes made it spuddery;
And when it rained, what muddery!

June days grow long and shaddery;
Bullfrog forgets his taddery;
The spider legs his laddery.

With cabbages so odory,
Snapdragon soon explodery,
At twilight all is toadery.

Young corn still far from foddery
No sign of goldenrodery,
Yet feeling low and doddery

Is poor old Mr. Bidery,
His garden lush and spidery,
His apples green, not cidery.

Pea-picking *is* so poddery!

David McCord

The Puffin

Upon this cake of ice is perched
The paddle-footed Puffin;
To find his double we have searched,
But have discovered—Nuffin!

Robert Williams Wood

Eletelephony

Once there was an elephant,
Who tried to use the telephant—
No! no! I mean an elephone
Who tried to use the telephone—
(Dear me! I am not certain quite
That even now I've got it right.)

Howe'er it was, he got his trunk
Entangled in the telephunk;
The more he tried to get it free,
The louder buzzed the telephee—
(I fear I'd better drop the song
Of elephop and telephong!)

Laura E. Richards

Sing Me a Song of Teapots and Trumpets

Sing me a song
of teapots and trumpets:
Trumpots and teapets
And tippets and taps,
trippers and trappers
and jelly bean wrappers
and pigs in pajamas
with zippers and snaps.

Sing me a song
of sneakers and snoopers:
Snookers and sneapers
and snappers and snacks,
snorkels and snarkles,
a seagull that gargles,
and gargoyles and gryphons
and other knickknacks.

Sing me a song
of parsnips and pickles:
and pumpkins and pears,
plumbers and mummers
and kettle drum drummers
and plum jam (yum-yum jam)
all over their chairs.

Sing me a song—
but never you mind it!
I've had enough
of this nonsense. Don't cry.
Criers and fliers
and onion ring fryers—
It's more than I want to put up with!
Good-by!

N. M. Bodecker

Banananananananana

I thought I'd win the spelling bee
    And get right to the top,
But I started to spell "banana,"
    And I didn't know when to stop.

William Cole

Clickbeetle

Click beetle
Clack beetle
Snapjack black beetle
Glint glitter glare beetle
Pin it in your hair beetle
Tack it to your shawl beetle
Wear it at the ball beetle
Shine shimmer spark beetle
Glisten in the dark beetle
Listen to it crack beetle
Click beetle
Clack beetle

Mary Ann Hoberman

The Ptarmigan

The ptarmigan is strange,
As strange as he can be;
Never sits on ptelephone poles
Or roosts upon a ptree.
And the way he ptakes pto spelling
Is the strangest thing pto me.

Anonymous

Misnomer

If you've ever been one
you know that
you don't sit the baby,
you bouncer
stander
holder
halter
puller
patter
rocker
feeder
burper
changer
kisser
bedder

Eve Merriam

The Modern Hiawatha

He killed the noble Mudjokivis;
With the skin he made him mittens,
Made them with the fur side inside,
Made them with the skin side outside,
He, to get the warm side inside,
Put the inside skin side outside:
He, to get the cold side outside,
Put the warm side fur side inside:
That's why he put the fur side inside,
Why he put the skin side outside,
Why he turned them inside outside.

George A. Strong

To Be or Not To Be

I sometimes think I'd rather crow
And be a rooster than to roost
And be a crow. But I dunno.

A rooster he can roost also,
Which don't seem fair when crows can't crow.
Which may help, some. Still I dunno.

Crows should be glad of one thing, though;
Nobody thinks of eating crow,
While roosters they are good enough
For anyone unless they're tough.

There are lots of tough old roosters though,
And anyway a crow can't crow,
So mebby roosters stand more show.
It looks that way. But I dunno.

Anonymous

Wild Flowers

"Of what are you afraid, my child?" inquired the kindly teacher.
"Oh, sir! the flowers, they are wild," replied the timid creature.

Peter Newell

Don't Ever Seize
a Weasel by the Tail

You should never squeeze a weasel
for you might displease the weasel,
and don't ever seize a weasel by the tail.

Let his tail blow in the breeze;
if you pull it, he will sneeze,
for the weasel's constitution tends to be a little frail.

Yes the weasel wheezes easily;
the weasel freezes easily;
the weasel's tan complexion rather suddenly turns pale.

So don't displease or tease a weasel,
squeeze or freeze or wheeze a weasel
and don't ever seize a weasel by the tail.

Jack Prelutsky

Have You Ever Seen?

Have you ever seen a sheet on a river bed?
Or a single hair from a hammer's head?
Has the foot of a mountain any toes?
And is there a pair of garden hose?

Does the needle ever wink its eye?
Why doesn't the wing of a building fly?
Can you tickle the ribs of a parasol?
Or open the trunk of a tree at all?

Are the teeth of a rake ever going to bite?
Have the hands of a clock any left or right?
Can the garden plot be deep and dark?
And what is the sound of the birch's bark?

Anonymous

An Atrocious Pun

A major, with wonderful force,
Called out in Hyde Park for a horse.
    All the flowers looked round,
    But no horse could be found,
So he just rhododendron, of course.

Anonymous

Waiters

Dining with his older daughter
Dad forgot to order water.
Daughter quickly called the waiter.
Waiter said he'd bring it later.
So she waited, did the daughter,
Till the waiter brought her water.
When he poured it for her later,
Which one would you call the waiter?

Mary Ann Hoberman

J's the Jumping Jay-Walker

J's the jumping Jay-walker,
   A sort of human jeep.
He crosses where the lights are red.
   Before he looks, he'll leap!
Then many a wheel
Begins to squeal,
   And many a brake to slam.
He turns your knees to jelly
   And the traffic into jam.

Phyllis McGinley

Poetry

What is Poetry? Who knows?
Not a rose, but the scent of the rose;
Not the sky, but the light in the sky;
Not the fly, but the gleam of the fly;
Not the sea, but the sound of the sea;
Not myself, but what makes me
See, hear, and feel something that prose
Cannot: and what it is, who knows?

Eleanor Farjeon

Lumps

Humps are lumps
and so are mumps.

Bumps make lumps
on heads.

Mushrooms grow
in clumps of lumps—
on clumps of stumps,
in woods and dumps.

Springs spring lumps
in beds.

Mosquito bites
make itchy lumps.

Frogs on logs
make twitchy lumps.

Judith Thurman

A Word

A word is dead
When it is said,
   Some say.

I say it just
Begins to live
   That day.

Emily Dickinson

Feelings About Words

Some words clink
As ice in drink.
Some move with grace
A dance, a lace.
Some sound thin:
Wail, scream and pin.
Some words are squat:
A mug, a pot,
And some are plump,
Fat, round and dump.
Some words are light:
Drift, lift and bright.
A few are small:
A, is and all.
And some are thick,
Glue, paste and brick.
Some words are sad:
"I never had. . . ."
And others gay:
Joy, spin and play.
Some words are sick:
Stab, scratch and nick.
Some words are hot:
Fire, flame and shot.
Some words are sharp,
Sword, point and carp.
And some alert:
Glint, glance and flirt.
Some words are lazy:
Saunter, hazy.
And some words preen:
Pride, pomp and queen.
Some words are quick,
A jerk, a flick.
Some words are slow:
Lag, stop and grow,
While others poke
As ox with yoke.
Some words can fly—
There's wind, there's high;
And some words cry:
"Goodbye . . .
Goodbye. . . ."

Mary O'Neill

The Yak

Yickity-yackity, yickity-yak,
the yak has a scriffily, scraffily back;
some yaks are brown yaks and some yaks are black,
yickity-yackity, yickity-yak.

Sniggildy-snaggildy, sniggildy-snag,
the yak is all covered with shiggildy-shag;
he walks with a ziggildy-zaggildy-zag,
sniggildy-snaggildy, sniggildy-snag.

Yickity-yackity, yickity-yak,
the yak has a scriffily, scraffily back;
some yaks are brown and some yaks are black,
yickity-yackity, yickity-yak.

Jack Prelutsky

WHERE GOBLINS DWELL

There is a place where goblins dwell,
where leprechauns abound,
where evil trolls inhabit holes,
and elves are often found,
where unicorns grow silver horns,
and mummies leave their tombs,
where fiery hosts of ashen ghosts
cavort in drafty rooms.

There is a place where poltergeists
and ogres rove unseen,
where witches rise through midnight skies,
where stalks the phantom queen,
where fairy folk atop an oak
are apt to weave a spell;
it's there to find within your mind,
that place where goblins dwell.

Some One

Some one came knocking
   At my wee, small door;
Some one came knocking,
   I'm sure—sure—sure;
I listened, I opened,
   I looked to left and right,
But naught there was a-stirring
   In the still dark night;
Only the busy beetle
   Tap-tapping in the wall,
Only from the forest
   The screech-owl's call,
Only the cricket whistling
   While the dewdrops fall,
So I know not who came knocking,
   At all, at all, at all.

Walter de la Mare

Something Is There

Something is there
   there on the stair
      coming down
         coming down
            stepping with care.
         Coming down
           coming down
             slinkety-sly.

Something is coming and wants to get by.

Lilian Moore

Ghosts

A cold and starry darkness moans
   And settles wide and still
Over a jumble of tumbled stones
   Dark on a darker hill.

An owl among those shadowy walls,
   Gray against the gray
Of ruins and brittle weeds, calls
   And soundless swoops away.

Rustling over scattered stones
   Dancers hover and sway,
Drifting among their own bones
   Like webs of the Milky Way.

Harry Behn

The Horseman

I heard a horseman
   Ride over the hill;
The moon shone clear,
The night was still;
His helm was silver,
   And pale was he;
And the horse he rode
   Was of ivory.

Walter de la Mare

hist whist

hist   whist
little ghostthings
tip-toe
twinkle-toe

little twitchy
witches and tingling
goblins
hob-a-nob   hob-a-nob

little hoppy happy
toad in tweeds
tweeds
little itchy mousies

with scuttling
eyes   rustle and run   and
hidehidehide
whisk

whisk   look out for the old woman
with the wart on her nose
what she'll do to yer
nobody knows

for she knows the devil   ooch
the devil   ouch
the devil
ach   the great

green
dancing
devil
devil

devil
devil

            wheeEEE

e. e. cummings

Green Candles

"There's someone at the door," said gold candlestick:
"Let her in quick, let her in quick!"
"There is a small hand groping at the handle.
Why don't you turn it!" asked green candle.

"Don't go, don't go," said the Hepplewhite chair,
"Lest you find a strange lady there."
"Yes, stay where you are," whispered the white wall:
"There is nobody there at all."

"I know her little foot," gray carpet said:
"Who but I should know her light tread?"
"She shall come in," answered the open door,
"And not," said the room, "go out anymore."

Humbert Wolfe

What's That?

What's that?
Who's there?
There's a great huge horrible *horrible*
creeping up the stair!
A huge big terrible *terrible*
with creepy crawly hair!
There's a ghastly grisly *ghastly*
with seven slimy eyes!
And flabby grabby tentacles
of a gigantic size!
He's crept into my room now,
he's leaning over me.
I wonder if he's thinking
how delicious I will be.

Florence Parry Heide

The Witch! The Witch!

The Witch! the Witch! don't let her get you!
Or your Aunt wouldn't know you the next time she met
    you!

Eleanor Farjeon

Song of the Witches

Double, double toil and trouble;
Fire burn and caldron bubble.
Fillet of a fenny snake,
In the caldron boil and bake;
Eye of newt and toe of frog,
Wool of bat and tongue of dog,
Adder's fork and blind-worm's sting,
Lizard's leg and howlet's wing,
For a charm of powerful trouble,
Like a hell-broth boil and bubble.

Double, double toil and trouble;
Fire burn and caldron bubble.
Cool it with a baboon's blood,
Then the charm is firm and good.

Macbeth: IV. i. 10–19; 35–38
William Shakespeare

Owl

On Midsummer night the witches shriek,
The frightened fairies swoon,
The nightjar mutters in his sleep
And ghosts around the chimney creep.
The loud winds cry, the fir trees crash,
And the owl stares at the moon.

Sylvia Read

Wanted—A Witch's Cat

Wanted—a witch's cat.
Must have vigor and spite,
Be expert at hissing,
And good in a fight,
And have balance and poise
On a broomstick at night.

Wanted—a witch's cat.
Must have hypnotic eyes
To tantalize victims
And mesmerize spies,
And be an adept
At scanning the skies.

Wanted—a witch's cat,
With a sly, cunning smile,
A knowledge of spells
And a good deal of guile,
With a fairly hot temper
And plenty of bile.

Wanted—a witch's cat,
Who's not afraid to fly,
For a cat with strong nerves
The salary's high
Wanted—a witch's cat;
Only the best need apply.

Shelagh McGee

Queen Nefertiti

Spin a coin, spin a coin,
  All fall down;
Queen Nefertiti
  Stalks through the town.

Over the pavements
  Her feet go clack
Her legs are as tall
  As a chimney stack;

Her fingers flicker
  Like snakes in the air,
The walls split open
  At her green-eyed stare;

Her voice is thin
  As the ghosts of bees;
She will crumble your bones,
  She will make your blood freeze.

Spin a coin, spin a coin,
  All fall down;
Queen Nefertiti
  Stalks through the town.

Anonymous

Witches' Menu

Live lizard; dead lizard
Marinated; fried.
Poached lizard; pickled lizard
Salty lizard hide.

Hot lizard, cold lizard
Lizard over ice.
Baked lizard, boiled lizard
Lizard served with spice.

Sweet lizard, sour lizard
Smoked lizard heart.
Leg of lizard, loin of lizard
Lizard a la carte.

Sonja Nikolay

Eight Witches

Eight witches rode the midnight sky.
One wailed low, and one wailed high,
Another croaked, another sighed
Throughout the eerie midnight ride.

One witch's voice was cackly toned,
Another shrieked, another moaned.
The eighth, much younger than the rest,
Made a scary sound the best—
Yoooo—

  Yoooo—

    Yoooo—

      Yoooo—

B. J. Lee

Colonel Fazackerley

Colonel Fazackerley Butterworth-Toast
Bought an old castle complete with a ghost,
But someone or other forgot to declare
To Colonel Fazack that the specter was there.

On the very first evening, while waiting to dine,
The Colonel was taking a fine sherry wine,
When the ghost, with a furious flash and a flare,
Shot out of the chimney and shivered, "Beware!"

Colonel Fazackerley put down his glass
And said, "My dear fellow, that's really first class!
I just can't conceive how you do it at all.
I imagine you're going to a Fancy Dress Ball?"

At this, the dread ghost gave a withering cry.
Said the Colonel (his monocle firm in his eye),
"Now just how you do it I wish I could think.
Do sit down and tell me, and please have a drink."

The ghost in his phosphorous cloak gave a roar
And floated about between ceiling and floor.
He walked through a wall and returned through a pane
And backed up the chimney and came down again.

Said the Colonel, "With laughter I'm feeling quite weak!"
(As trickles of merriment ran down his cheek).
"My house-warming party I hope you won't spurn.
You *must* say you'll come and you'll give us a turn!"

At this, the poor specter—quite out of his wits—
Proceeded to shake himself almost to bits.
He rattled his chains and he clattered his bones
And he filled the whole castle with mumbles and moans.

But Colonel Fazackerley, just as before,
Was simply delighted and called out, "Encore!"
At which the ghost vanished, his efforts in vain,
And never was seen at the castle again.

"Oh dear, what a pity!" said Colonel Fazack.
"I don't know his name, so I can't call him back."
And then with a smile that was hard to define,
Colonel Fazackerley went in to dine.

Charles Causley

Three Ghostesses

Three little ghostesses,
Sitting on postesses,
Eating buttered toastesses,
Greasing their fistesses,
Up to their wristesses,
Oh, what beastesses
To make such feastesses!

Anonymous

Song of the Ogres

Little fellow, you're amusing,
Stop before you end by losing
    Your shirt:
Run along to Mother, Gus,
Those who interfere with us
    Get hurt.

Honest Virtue, old wives prattle,
Always wins the final battle.
    Dear, Dear!
Life's exactly what it looks,
Love may triumph in the books,
    Not here.

We're not joking, we assure you:
Those who rode this way before you
    Died hard.
What? Still spoiling for a fight?
Well, you've asked for it all right:
    On guard!

Always hopeful, aren't you? Don't be.
Night is falling and it won't be
    Long now:
You will never see the dawn,
You will wish you'd not been born.
    And how!

W. H. Auden

The Darkling Elves

In wildest woods, on treetop shelves,
sit evil beings with evil selves—
they are the dreaded darkling elves
and they are always hungry.

In garish garb of capes and hoods,
they wait and watch within their woods
to peel your flesh and steal your goods
for they are always hungry.

Through brightest days and darkest nights
these terrifying tiny sprites
await to strike and take their bites
for they are always hungry.

Watch every leaf of every tree,
for once they pounce you cannot flee—
their teeth are sharp as sharp can be . . .
and they are always hungry.

Jack Prelutsky

The Elf and the Dormouse

Under a toadstool
   Crept a wee Elf,
Out of the rain
   To shelter himself.

Under the toadstool,
   Sound asleep,
Sat a big Dormouse
   All in a heap.

Trembled the wee Elf,
   Frightened, and yet
Fearing to fly away
   Lest he get wet.

To the next shelter—
   Maybe a mile!
Sudden the wee Elf
   Smiled a wee smile,

Tugged till the toadstool
   Toppled in two.
Holding it over him
   Gaily he flew.

Soon he was safe home
   Dry as could be.
Soon woke the Dormouse—
   "Good gracious me!

Where is my toadstool?"
   Loud he lamented.
   —And that's how umbrellas
First were invented.

Oliver Herford

The Bogeyman

In the desolate depths of a perilous place
the bogeyman lurks, with a snarl on his face.
Never dare, never dare to approach his dark lair
for he's waiting . . . just waiting . . . to get you.

He skulks in the shadows, relentless and wild
in his search for a tender, delectable child.
With his steely sharp claws and his slavering jaws
oh he's waiting . . . just waiting . . . to get you.

Many have entered his dreary domain
but not even one has been heard from again.
They no doubt made a feast for the butchering beast
and he's waiting . . . just waiting . . . to get you.

In that sulphurous, sunless and sinister place
he'll crumple your bones in his bogey embrace.
Never never go near if you hold your life dear,
for oh! . . . what he'll do . . . when he gets you!

Jack Prelutsky

The Troll

Be wary of the loathsome troll
that slyly lies in wait
to drag you to his dingy hole
and put you on his plate.

His blood is black and boiling hot,
he gurgles ghastly groans.
He'll cook you in his dinner pot,
your skin, your flesh, your bones.

He'll catch your arms and clutch your legs
and grind you to a pulp,
then swallow you like scrambled eggs—
gobble! gobble! gulp!

So watch your steps when next you go
upon a pleasant stroll,
or you might end in the pit below
as supper for the troll.

Jack Prelutsky

The Wendigo

The Wendigo,
The Wendigo!
Its eyes are ice and indigo!
Its blood is rank and yellowish!
Its voice is hoarse and bellowish!
Its tentacles are slithery,
And scummy,
Slimy,
Leathery!
Its lips are hungry blubbery,
And smacky,
Sucky,
Rubbery!

The Wendigo,
The Wendigo!
I saw it just a friend ago!
Last night it lurked in Canada;
Tonight, on your veranada!
As you are lolling hammockwise
It contemplates you stomachwise.
You loll,
It contemplates,
It lollops.
The rest is merely gulps and gollops.

Ogden Nash

Father and Mother

My father's name is Frankenstein,
He comes from the Barbados.
He fashioned me from package twine
And instant mashed potatoes.

My mother's name is Draculeen,
She lets a big bat bite her,
And folks who sleep here overnight
Wake up a few quarts lighter.

X. J. Kennedy

The Fairies

Up the airy mountain,
   Down the rushy glen,
We daren't go a-hunting
   For fear of little men;
Wee folk, good folk,
   Trooping all together;
Green jacket, red cap,
   And white owl's feather!

Down along the rocky shore
   Some make their home—
They live on crispy pancakes
   Of yellow tide-foam;
Some in the reeds
   Of the black mountain lake,
With frogs for their watch-dogs,
   All night awake.

By the craggy hillside,
   Through the mosses bare,
They have planted thorn-trees
   For pleasure here and there.
Is any man so daring
   As dig one up in spite,
He shall find their sharpest thorns
   In his bed at night.

Up the airy mountain,
   Down the rushy glen,
We daren't go a-hunting
   For fear of little men;
Wee folk, good folk,
   Trooping all together;
Green jacket, red cap,
   And white owl's feather!

William Allingham

The Great Auk's Ghost

The Great Auk's ghost rose on one leg,
  Sighed thrice and three times winked,
And turned and poached a phantom egg,
  And muttered, "I'm extinct."

Ralph Hodgson

The Pumpkin

You may not believe it, for hardly could I:
I was cutting a pumpkin to put in a pie,
And on it was written in letters most plain
"You may hack me in slices, but I'll grow
    again."

I seized it and sliced it and made no mistake
As, with dough rounded over, I put it to bake:
But soon in the garden as I chanced to walk,
Why, there was that pumpkin entire on his
    stalk!

Robert Graves

The Seven Ages of Elf-hood

When an Elf is as old as a year and a minute
He can wear a cap with a feather in it.

By the time that he is two times two
He has a buckle for either shoe.

At twenty he is fine as a fiddle,
With a little brown belt to go round his middle

When he's lived for fifty years or so
His coat may have buttons all in a row.

If past three score and ten he's grown
Two pockets he has for his very own.

At eighty-two or three years old
They bulge and jingle with bits of gold.

But when he's a hundred and a day
He gets a little pipe to play!

Rachel Field

How to Tell Goblins from Elves

The Goblin has a wider mouth
　　Than any wondering elf.
The saddest part of this is that
　　He brings it on himself.
For hanging in a willow clump
　　In baskets made of sheaves,
You may see the baby goblins
　　Under coverlets of leaves.

They suck a pink and podgy foot
　　(As human babies do),
And then they suck the other one,
　　Until they're sucking two.
And so it is that goblins' mouths
　　Keep growing very round.
So you can't mistake a goblin,
　　When a goblin you have found.

Monica Shannon

Unicorn

The Unicorn with the long white horn
　　Is beautiful and wild.
He gallops across the forest green
So quickly that he's seldom seen
Where Peacocks their blue feathers preen
　　And strawberries grow wild.
He flees the hunter and the hounds,
Upon black earth his white hoof pounds,
Over cold mountain streams he bounds
　　And comes to a meadow mild;
There, when he kneels to take his nap,
He lays his head in a lady's lap
　　As gently as a child.

William Jay Smith

Slithergadee

The Slithergadee has crawled out of the sea.
He may catch all the others, but he won't catch me.
No you won't catch me, old Slithergadee,
You may catch all the others, but you wo——

Shel Silverstein

Gumble

The Gumble lives behind the door;
At night he's oft inclined to snore,
Waking me in such a fright
I leap from bed, turn on the light,
And clad in dressing gown and slippers
Drag out the Gumble by his flippers,
Admonish him with such a smack
He first turns blue and then turns black,
While I, ashamed at what I've done,
Go back to bed and count to one
Thousand and three Gumblish sheep
In vain attempt to go to sleep,
While Gumble sniggers, "Serves him right,
I hope he's kept awake all night."

Michael Dugan

The Little Man

As I was walking up the stair
I met a man who wasn't there;
He wasn't there again today.
I wish, I wish he'd stay away.

Hughes Mearns

The Bogus-Boo

The Bogus-boo
Is a creature who
Comes out at night—and why?
He likes the air;
He likes to scare
The nervous passer-by.

Out from the park
At dead of dark
He comes with huffling pad.
If, when alone,
You hear his moan,
'Tis like to drive you mad.

He has two wings,
Pathetic things,
With which he cannot fly.
His tusks look fierce,
Yet could not pierce
The merest butterfly.

He has six ears,
But what he hears
Is very faint and small;
And with the claws
On his eight paws
He cannot scratch at all.

He looks so wise
With his owl-eyes,
His aspect grim and ghoulish;
But truth to tell,
He sees not well
And is distinctly foolish.

This Bogus-boo,
What can he do
But huffle in the dark?
So don't take fright;
He has no bite
And very little bark.

James Reeves

Wrimples

When the clock strikes five but it's only four,
there's a wrimple in your clock.
When your key won't work in your own front door,
there's a wrimple in the lock.

When your brand-new shoes refuse to fit,
there's a wrimple in each shoe.
When the lights go out and they just were lit,
that's a wrimple's doing too.

When you shake and shake but the salt won't pour,
there's a wrimple in the salt.
When your cake falls flat on the kitchen floor,
it's surely a wrimple's fault.

The way to fix these irksome works
is obvious and simple.
Just search and find it where it lurks,
and then . . . remove the wrimple.

Jack Prelutsky

Ms. Whatchamacallit Thingamajig

Ms. Whatchamacallit Thingamajig
can make herself small or make herself big,
can take any shape, from round as a ball
to sharp as a spear, to wide as a wall.

She makes no sound as she creeps, flies or shakes
(how she moves depends on the shape that she takes).
And though she is soundless, she's always around.
Wherever you are—there she can be found.

What? You've never seen her? That's because she's
invisible by day and disguised as a breeze.
At night, when the lights are out in the house,
she takes on the shape of a shadow or mouse.

Though you've never seen her, she's always close by.
Have you never felt something fly in your eye?
Or noticed the cat stare at someone unseen?
Or found dirt on a shirt that was utterly clean?

Have you ever been pushed and found no one there?
Or dropped a glass you were holding with care?
What of itches, tickles, scratches and those?
Are they all just—accidents—do you suppose?

You have the idea. You're beginning to see.
Yes, those are the doings of Ms. W. T.
She loves a good laugh, and laughs without end
to see a look of surprise on the face of a friend.

Miriam Chaikin

The Spangled Pandemonium

The Spangled Pandemonium
Is missing from the zoo.
He bent the bars the barest bit,
And slithered glibly through.

He crawled across the moated wall,
He climbed the mango tree,
And when his keeper scrambled up,
He nipped him in the knee.

To all of you, a warning
Not to wander after dark,
Or if you must, make very sure
You stay out of the park.

For the Spangled Pandemonium
Is missing from the zoo,
And since he nipped his keeper,
He would just as soon nip you!

Palmer Brown

The Creature in the Classroom

It appeared inside our classroom
at a quarter after ten,
it gobbled up the blackboard,
three erasers and a pen.
It gobbled teacher's apple
and it bopped her with the core.
"How dare you!" she responded.
"You must leave us . . . there's the door."

The Creature didn't listen
but described an arabesque
as it gobbled all her pencils,
seven notebooks and her desk.
Teacher stated very calmly,
"Sir! You simply cannot stay,
I'll report you to the principal
unless you go away!"

But the thing continued eating,
it ate paper, swallowed ink,
as it gobbled up our homework
I believe I saw it wink.
Teacher finally lost her temper.
"OUT!" she shouted at the creature.
The creature hopped beside her
and GLOPP . . . it swallowed teacher.

Jack Prelutsky

Dinky

O what's the weather in a Beard?
It's windy there, and rather weird,
And when you think the sky has cleared
   —Why, there is Dirty Dinky.

Suppose you walk out in a Storm,
With nothing on to keep you warm,
And then step barefoot on a Worm
   —Of course, it's Dirty Dinky.

As I was crossing a hot hot Plain,
I saw a sight that caused me pain,
You asked me before,
I'll tell you again:
   —It *looked* like Dirty Dinky.

Last night you lay a-sleeping?
No! The room was thirty-five below;
The sheets and blankets turned to snow
   —He'd got in: Dirty Dinky.

You'd better watch the things you do,
You'd better watch the things you do.
You're part of him; he's part of you
   —*You* may be Dirty Dinky.

Theodore Roethke

Could It Have Been a Shadow?

What ran under the rosebush?
    What ran under the stone?
Could it have been a shadow,
    Running away alone?
Maybe a fairy's shadow,
    Slipping away at dawn
To guard a gleaming pot of gold
    For a busy leprechaun.

Monica Shannon

The Plumpuppets

When little heads weary have gone to their bed,
When all the good nights and the prayers have been said,
Of all the good fairies that send bairns to rest
The little Plumpuppets are those I love best.

If your pillow is lumpy, or hot, thin and flat,
The little Plumpuppets know just what they're at;
They plump up the pillow, all soft, cool and fat—
    The little Plumpuppets plump-up it!

The little Plumpuppets are fairies of beds:
They have nothing to do but to watch sleepy heads;
They turn down the sheets and they tuck you in tight,
And they dance on your pillow to wish you good night!

No matter what troubles have bothered the day,
Though your doll broke her arm or the pup ran away;
Though your handies are black with the ink that was spilt—
Plumpuppets are waiting in blankets and quilt.

If your pillow is lumpy, or hot, thin and flat,
The little Plumpuppets know just what they're at;
They plump up the pillow; all soft, cool and fat—
    The little Plumpuppets plump-up it!

Christopher Morley

THE LAND OF POTPOURRI

Oh, take my hand and stroll with me
into the Land of Potpourri,
a land to think, a land to dream,
a land of peaches topped with cream,
of orange crayons, yellow pears,
a wind-up frog upon the stairs,
a windy beach, a flying bed,
a helicopter overhead.

In Potpourri you're sure to spy
a locomotive clacking by,
a toaster pop, a rocket roar,
a shovel like a dinosaur,
a puzzled mouse in outer space,
a breathless theft of second base;
so take my hand and stroll with me
into the Land of Potpourri.

Our Washing Machine

Our washing machine went whisity whirr
Whisity whisity whisity whirr
One day at noon it went whisity click
Whisity whisity whisity click
Click grr click grr click grr click
    Call the repairman
    Fix it . . . Quick!

Patricia Hubbell

Steam Shovel

The dinosaurs are not all dead.
I saw one raise its iron head
To watch me walking down the road
Beyond our house today.
Its jaws were dripping with a load
Of earth and grass that it had cropped.
It must have heard me where I stopped,
Snorted white steam my way,
And stretched its long neck out to see,
And chewed, and grinned quite amiably.

Charles Malam

Happy Thought

The world is so full of a number of things,
I'm sure we should all be as happy as kings.

Robert Louis Stevenson

Introduction
to Songs of Innocence

Piping down the valleys wild,
    Piping songs of pleasant glee,
On a cloud I saw a child,
    And he laughing said to me:

"Pipe a song about a Lamb!"
    So I piped with merry cheer.
"Piper, pipe that song again";
    So I piped; he wept to hear.

"Drop thy pipe, thy happy pipe;
    Sing thy songs of happy cheer!"
So I sang the same again,
    While he wept with joy to hear.

"Piper, sit thee down and write
    In a book, that all may read."
So he vanished from my sight;
    And I plucked a hollow reed,

And I made a rural pen,
    And I stained the water clear,
And I wrote my happy songs
    Every child may joy to hear.

William Blake

No Holes Marred

For printed instructions
    I had a great regard,
Until, in the mail,
    Came an IBM card
With a written command
    Not to crease it or fold it,
And a stamped, return envelope—
    Too small to hold it.

Suzanne Douglass

From: The Bed Book

These are the Beds
for me and for you!
These are the Beds
to climb into:

Pocket-size Beds
and Beds for Snacks,
Tank Beds, Beds
on Elephant Backs,
Beds that fly,
or go under water,
Bouncy Beds, Beds
you can spatter and spotter,
Bird-Watching Beds,
Beds for Zero Weather—
any kind of Bed
as long as it's rather
special and queer
and full of surprises,

Beds of amazing
shapes and sizes—
NOT just a white little
tucked-in-tight little
nighty-night little
turn-out-the-light little
    bed!

Sylvia Plath

The Toaster

A silver-scaled Dragon with jaws flaming red
Sits at my elbow and toasts my bread.
I hand him fat slices, and then, one by one,
He hands them back when he sees they are done.

William Jay Smith

Driving to the Beach

On the road
smell fumes and tar
through the windows
of the car.

But at the beach
smell suntan lotion
and wind
    and sun
        and ocean!

Joanna Cole

My Nose

It doesn't breathe;
It doesn't smell;
It doesn't feel
So very well.

I am discouraged
With my nose:
The only thing it
Does is blows.

Dorothy Aldis

The Tin Frog

I have hopped, when properly wound up, the whole length
Of the hallway; once hopped halfway down the stairs, and fell.
Since then the two halves of my tin have been awry; my strength
Is not quite what it used to be; I do not hop so well.

Russell Hoban

Arithmetic

Arithmetic is where numbers fly
   like pigeons in and out of your head.
Arithmetic tells you how many you lose or win
   if you know how many you had
   before you lost or won.
Arithmetic is seven eleven all good children
   go to heaven—or five six bundle of sticks.
Arithmetic is numbers you squeeze from your
   head to your hand to your pencil to your paper
   till you get the right answer. . . .
If you have two animal crackers, one good and one bad,
   and you eat one and a striped zebra
   with streaks all over him eats the other,
   how many animal crackers will you have
   if somebody offers you five six seven and you say
   No no no and you say Nay nay nay
   and you say Nix nix nix?
 If you ask your mother for one fried egg
   for breakfast and she gives you
   two fried eggs and you eat
   both of them, who is better in arithmetic,
   you or your mother?

Carl Sandburg

What Is Pink?

What is pink? A rose is pink
By the fountain's brink.
What is red? A poppy's red
In its barley bed.
What is blue? The sky is blue
Where the clouds float through.
What is white? A swan is white
Sailing in the light.
What is yellow? Pears are yellow,
Rich and ripe and mellow.
What is green? The grass is green,
With small flowers between.
What is violet? Clouds are violet
In the summer twilight.
What is orange? Why, an orange,
Just an orange!

Christina Rossetti

What Is Orange?

Orange is a tiger lily,
A carrot,
A feather from
A parrot,
A flame,
The wildest color
You can name.
Orange is a happy day
Saying good-by
In a sunset that
Shocks the sky.
Orange is brave
Orange is bold
It's bittersweet
And marigold.
Orange is zip
Orange is dash
The brightest stripe
In a Roman sash.
Orange is an orange
Also a mango
Orange is music
Of the tango.
Orange is the fur
Of the fiery fox,
The brightest crayon
In the box.
And in the fall
When the leaves are turni
Orange is the smell
Of a bonfire burning. . . .

Mary O'Neill

Who's In

"The door is shut fast
And everyone's out."
But people don't know
What they're talking about!
Says the fly on the wall,
And the flame on the coals
And the dog on his rug
And the mice in their holes,
And the kitten curled up,
And the spiders that spin—
"What, everyone's out?
Why, everyone's in!"

Elizabeth Fleming

The Base Stealer

Poised between going on and back, pulled
Both ways taut like a tightrope-walker,
Fingertips pointing the opposites,
Now bouncing tiptoe like a dropped ball
Or a kid skipping rope, come on, come on,
Running a scattering of steps sidewise,
How he teeters, skitters, tingles, teases,
Taunts them, hovers like an ecstatic bird,
He's only flirting, crowd him, crowd him,
Delicate, delicate, delicate, delicate—now!

Robert Francis

To Be Answered in Our Next Issue

When a great tree falls
And people aren't near,
Does it make a noise
If no one can hear?
And which came first,
The hen or the egg?
This impractical question
We ask and then beg.
Some wise men say
It's beyond their ken.
Did anyone ever
Ask the hen?

Anonymous

What Is Red?

Red is a sunset
Blazy and bright.
Red is feeling brave
With all your might.
Red is a sunburn
Spot on your nose,
Sometimes red
Is a red, red rose.
Red squiggles out
When you cut your hand.
Red is a brick and
A rubber band.
Red is a hotness
You get inside
When you're embarrassed
And want to hide.
Fire-cracker, fire-engine
Fire-flicker red—
And when you're angry
Red runs through your head.
Red is an Indian,
A Valentine heart,
The trimming on
A circus cart.
Red is a lipstick,
Red is a shout,
Red is a signal
That says: "Watch out!"
Red is a great big
Rubber ball.
Red is the giant-est
Color of all.
Red is a show-off
No doubt about it—
But can you imagine
Living without it?

Mary O'Neill

The Library

It looks like any building
When you pass it on the street,
Made of stone and glass and marble,
Made of iron and concrete.

But once inside you can ride
A camel or a train,
Visit Rome, Siam, or Nome,
Feel a hurricane,
Meet a king, learn to sing,
How to bake a pie,
Go to sea, plant a tree,
Find how airplanes fly,
Train a horse, and of course
Have all the dogs you'd like,
See the moon, a sandy dune,
Or catch a whopping pike.
Everything that books can bring
You'll find inside those walls.
A world is there for you to share
When adventure calls.

You cannot tell its magic
By the way the building looks,
But there's wonderment within it,
The wonderment of books.

Barbara A. Huff

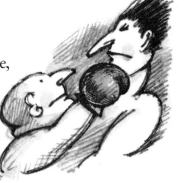

Yellow

Green is go,
and red is stop,
and yellow is peaches
with cream on top.

Earth is brown,
and blue is sky;
yellow looks well
on a butterfly.

Clouds are white,
black, pink, or mocha;
yellow's a dish of
tapioca.

David McCord

The Knockout

The shortest fight
I ever saw
Was a left to the body
And a right to the jaw.

Lillian Morrison

Foul Shot

With two 60's stuck on the scoreboard
And two seconds hanging on the clock
The solemn boy in the center of eyes,
Squeezed by silence,
Seeks out the line with his feet,
Soothes his hands along his uniform,
Gently drums the ball against the floor
Then measures the waiting net,
Raises the ball on his right hand,
Balances it with his left,
Calms it with fingertips,
Breathes,
Crouches,
Waits,
And then through a stretching of stilln
Nudges it upward.

The ball slides up and out.
Lands,
Leans,
Wobbles,
Wavers,
Hesitates,
Exasperates,
Plays it coy
Until every face begs with unsounding
        screams—
And then
      And then,
           And then,
Right before ROAR-UP,
Dives down and through.

Edwin A. Ho

A Football Game

It's the might, it's the fight
    Of two teams who won't give in—
It's the roar of the crowd
    And the "Go, fight, win!"

It's the bands, it's the stands,
    It's the color everywhere.
It's the whiff, it's the sniff
    Of the popcorn on the air.
It's a thrill, it's a chill,
    It's a cheer and then a sigh;
It's that deep, breathless hush
    When the ball soars high.

Yes, it's more than a score,
    Or a desperate grasp at fame;
Fun is King, win or lose—
    That's a football game!

Alice Van Eck

If Once You Have Slept on an Island

If once you have slept on an island
    You'll never be quite the same;
You may look as you looked the day before
    And go by the same old name,

You may bustle about in street and shop;
    You may sit at home and sew,
But you'll see blue water and wheeling gulls
    Wherever your feet may go.

You may chat with the neighbors of this and that
    And close to your fire keep,
But you'll hear ship whistle and lighthouse bell
    And tides beat through your sleep.

Oh, you won't know why, and you can't say how
    Such change upon you came,
But—once you have slept on an island
    You'll never be quite the same!

Rachel Field

Maps

High adventure
    And bright dream—
Maps are mightier
    Than they seem:

Ships that follow
    Leaning stars—
Red and gold of
    Strange bazaars—

Ice floes hid
    Beyond all knowing—
Planes that ride where
    Winds are blowing!

Train maps, maps of
    Wind and weather,
Road maps—taken
    Altogether

Maps are really
    Magic wands
For home-staying
    Vagabonds!

Dorothy Brown Thompson

Train Song

Out in back
railroad track
clickety-clack
clickety-clack
great trains
freight trains
talk about your late trains
the 509
right on time
straight through to L.A.
whistle blows
there she goes
slicing through the day.
Trains with faces in a row
going places: Buffalo
New York City, Boston, Mass.
slowing 'neath the underpass
engineers with striped hats
head-of-the-line aristocrats
up in front, sitting high,
wave at me as they go by
Southern Route
Sante Fe
Cotton Belt
on their way
boxcars
flatcars

going-to-North Platte cars
grain trains
Maine trains
going-through-the-rain trains
long trains
strong trains
singing-clickety-song trains
cars with lumber
cars with cattle
clickety-clacking
to Seattle.
Detroit to Chicago
departing at five
whenever we get there
is when we arrive.
Midnight special
to Cheyenne
get a sleeper
if you can
ALL ABOARD! say good-bye
hear the railroad lullaby.

Diane Siebert

Flight Plan

Of all the ways of traveling in earth and air and sea
It's the lively helicopter that has captivated me.
It hovers anywhere in air just like a hummingbird.
Flies backward; forward, up or down, whichever is preferred.
It doesn't pierce the stratosphere as zipping rockets do
Nor pop sound barriers and puff fat jet streams through the blue.
It isn't first in speed or weight or anything but fun
And deftly doing dangerous jobs that often must be done.
When anyone is lost in storm or flooded river's span
And other planes can't help at all, a helicopter can.
It lights on snow or mountaintop—wherever it is needed.
The plane that's like a hummingbird will not be superseded
By satellite or Stratojet. No supership has topped her.
And just as soon as ever I can I'll fly a helicopter!

Jane Merchant

To an Aviator

You who have grown so intimate with stars
And know their silver dripping from your wings,
Swept with the breaking day across the sky,
Known kinship with each meteor that swings—

You who have touched the rainbow's fragile gold,
Carved lyric ways through dawn and dusk and rain
And soared to heights our hearts have only dreamed—
How can you walk earth's common ways again?

Daniel Whitehead Hicky

Travel

The railroad track is miles away,
    And the day is loud with voices speaking,
Yet there isn't a train goes by all day
    But I hear its whistles shrieking.

All night there isn't a train goes by,
    Though the night is still for sleep and dreaming
But I see its cinders red on the sky
    And hear its engine steaming.

My heart is warm with the friends I make,
    And better friends I'll not be knowing,
Yet there isn't a train I wouldn't take,
    No matter where it's going.

Edna St. Vincent Millay

Message from a Mouse, Ascending in a Rocket

Attention, architect!
Attention, engineer!
A message from mouse,
Coming clear:

"Suggest installing
Spike or sprocket
Easily turned by
A mouse in a rocket;
An ejection gadget
Simple to handle
To free mouse quickly
From this space-age ramble.
Suggest packing
For the next moon trip
A mouse-sized parachute
Somewhere in the ship,
So I can descend
(When my fear comes strong)
Back to earth where I was born.
Back to the cheerful world of cheese
    And small mice playing,
    And my wife waiting."

Patricia Hubbell

From a Railway Carriage

Faster than fairies, faster than witches,
Bridges and houses, hedges and ditches;
And charging along like troops in a battle,
All through the meadows the horses and cattle:
All of the sights of the hill and the plain
Fly as thick as driving rain;
And ever again, in the wink of an eye,
Painted stations whistle by.

Here is a child who clambers and scrambles,
All by himself and gathering brambles;
Here is a tramp who stands and gazes;
And there is the green for stringing the daisies!

Here is a cart run away in the road
Lumping along with man and load;
And here is a mill and there is a river:
Each a glimpse and gone for ever!

Robert Louis Stevenson

The Toad

In days of old, those far off times
    Of high romance and magic,
A toad was an enchanted prince,
    A transformation tragic.

Today the toad is studied as
    A scientific topic—
No prince is found, although we look
    With vision microscopic.

And yet, the prince is there—he's there
    As clearly as can be.
Forget your microscope, my friend,
    And use your mind to see!

Robert S. Oliver

This Little Pig Built a Spaceship

This little pig built a spaceship,
  This little pig paid the bill;
This little pig made isotopes,
  This little pig ate a pill;
And this little pig did nothing at all,
  But he's just a little pig still.

Frederick Winsor

Dreams

Hold fast to dreams
For if dreams die
Life is a broken-winged bird
That cannot fly.

Hold fast to dreams
For when dreams go
Life is a barren field
Frozen with snow.

Langston Hughes

How Strange It Is

In the sky
Soft clouds are blowing by.
Nothing more can I see
In the blue air over me.

Yet I know that planetoids and rocket cones,
Telstars studded with blue stones,
And many hundred bits of fins
And other man-made odds and ends
Are wheeling round me out in space
At a breathless astronautic pace.

How strange it is to know
That while I watch the soft clouds blow
So many things I cannot see
Are passing by right over me.

Claudia Lewis

Far Trek

Some things will never change although
We tour out to the stars;
Arriving on the moon we'll find
Our luggage sent to Mars!

June Brady

226

The Paint Box

"Cobalt and umber and ultramarine,
Ivory black and emerald green—
What shall I paint to give pleasure to you?"
"Paint for me somebody utterly new."

"I have painted you tigers in crimson and white."
"The colors were good and you painted aright."
"I have painted the cook and a camel in blue
And a panther in purple." "You painted them true.

"Now mix me a color that nobody knows,
And paint me a country where nobody goes.
And put in it people a little like you,
Watching a unicorn drinking the dew."

E.V. Rieu

Keep a Poem in Your Pocket

Keep a poem in your pocket
and a picture in your head
and you'll never feel lonely
at night when you're in bed.

The little poem will sing to you
the little picture bring to you
a dozen dreams to dance to you
at night when you're in bed.

So—
Keep a picture in your pocket
and a poem in your head
and you'll never feel lonely
at night when you're in bed.

Beatrice Schenk de Regniers

To Dark Eyes Dreaming

Dreams go fast and far
these days.
They go by rocket thrust.
They go arrayed
in lights
or in the dust of stars.
Dreams, these days,
go fast and far.
Dreams are young, these days,
or very old,
They can be black
or blue or gold.
They need no special charts,
nor any fuel.
It seems, only one rule applies,
to all our dreams—
They will not fly except in open sky.
A fenced-in dream
will die.

Zilpha Keatley Snyder

INDEX OF TITLES

INDEX OF FIRST LINES

235

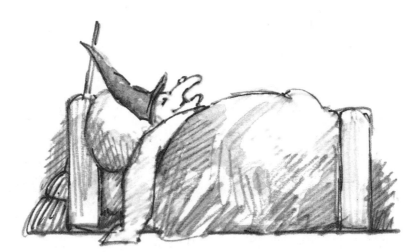

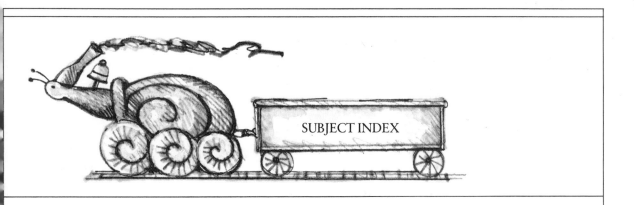

The following index supplements the table of contents at the beginning of this book. We hope that it will be helpful to *all* those who use this book—especially to teachers as a way of adding the fun and beauty of poetry to a variety of subjects in the school curriculum and to special events throughout the year. Creating this index was a selective process. We felt it would be more useful to list subjects that either reoccurred with frequency, such as spring, or highlighted a particular theme or concept, such as imagination, rather than to list every image that appeared in the poems.

The Editors

Jack Prelutsky's first collection of poems was published in 1967. His skill as a wordsmith who tickles young funnybones has been increasing with each new volume of his verse. There are now over thirty. Whether creating nonsensical portraits such as those in *The Queen of Eene* or exploring the dark world of *Nightmares,* Mr. Prelutsky creates rhyming images that never fail to delight his readers. Mr. Prelutsky spends much of his time presenting poems to children in schools and libraries throughout the United States. This constant contact with children and their mentors not only nourishes his own work, but it also gives him a keen awareness of poems children respond to and find relevant—knowledge that made him especially qualified to select poems for this anthology.

Arnold Lobel has been delighting children and the young at heart since he first started illustrating children's books in 1961. What he calls "the little world at the end of my pencil" reveals a gentle sense of humor and subtle sensitivity transmitted with craftsmanship. He has now illustrated over seventy books for children, some of which he wrote. Mr. Lobel received the Caldecott Medal for *Fables* in 1981. *Frog and Toad Are Friends* was a Caldecott Honor Book in 1971, and its sequel, *Frog and Toad Together,* was a 1973 Newbery Honor Book. *The Random House Book of Poetry for Children,* his most ambitious project to date, gives Mr. Lobel an infinite arena in which to display his virtuosity. Poems about nature, holidays, animals, the city, the supernatural—silly poems and serious poems—are all given an added dimension by his art.

A Note of Thanks

More people than space allows me to name helped make this book a reality. Although unmentioned, they are not unappreciated. I'd like to give special thanks to Janet Schulman at Random House, who recognized the need for a comprehensive new anthology for today's child and worked closely with me in making final choices, as well as Ole Risom, the art director; Jos. Trautwein, the designer; and Arnold Lobel, whose sensitive and exuberant illustrations embellish every page. I'd also like to thank Bill Cole and the many librarians who helped me track down poems and poets, and my wife, Carolynn, for her support. Most of all I'd like to thank the poets whose voices will continue to sing in celebration of life and childhood in this book.

Jack Prelutsky

A Note on the Type

The text of this book was set in Sabon, a typeface created by Jan Tschichold, the well-known German typographer.

The book was designed by Jos. Trautwein of Bentwood Studios.
Printed and bound by Krueger Company.